Beeep

An Almost True Tale

A novella
by
Tim Campbell

Beeep

© 2015 Timothy C. Campbell, Sr.
Published by Augusta-Heritage Press
@ www.augusta-heritagepress.com &
www.whitebeardbooks.com

ISBN: 979-8-9853860-0-4

Disclaimer:

Acknowledgements:

The unique cover art for this book is an original painting done by a fine young and talented artist Bridgette Petrie. Many thanks for her help.

Dedication

This book is dedicated with loving memory to my late brother,

David Crowther Campbell

NOTE: My brother was a career professional Firefighter and EMT, First Responder. The outdoor party scene early in this tale was the result of a birthday party held for his 77th, and it was there the story presented itself to me initially.

Prologue

I'm going to share a story with you about someone to whom I have the good fortune not only to meet but with whom I have the great pleasure to be related. You see, this tale is about two young ladies and one of them is my brother's great granddaughter. The other is within the first. I already know as I write these words, that when you read them your reaction will be 'right, sure, this is totally crazy and can't be true.' But let me assure you that I have seen all this first-hand and have experienced those moments that I have attempted to capture on these pages. So, if you jump to the conclusion that somehow it is me who has made the mistake, then accept the simple fact that the mistake is *yours*. While this tale is fantastic, you can believe every word. Why? Because I told you so. Now let's get on with the facts before us.

Chapter One

I would guess that it was more than a dozen years ago that I had the pleasure to meet a young lady by the name of Bridgette Eleece Padgette (okay, so I did alter the name slightly to maintain her privacy, because when this story gets out, she will be constantly harassed by the media and people who want favors and, well you can just imagine). Now when the young lady introduced herself to me, she gave me the complete moniker followed quickly by the note that her friends call her Beeep. She also added that it was spelled with a bunch of "e's" owing to the fact that her first initial is a B, and her middle name has those four "e's" and her last name has more "e's" and starts with a "P". Still, the nickname is pronounced the same as if it only had two "e's" in the middle.

I had the pleasure of knowing a really nice, dedicated student who later made me aware of the fact he had met my great niece while they were both students where I taught at the local university. Shortly after that academic year, they had married. Over the following few years, the three of us had regularly crossed paths and after graduation they developed a local business where I had been in a position to offer advice when they requested it. They now have two children, Jacob and Brigette.

Oh, I should also say that when first I met their daughter, Brigette, she appeared to be an early teenager. You know about thirteen or fourteen. And here comes the first of those 'ain't no way', but yes there is way! I saw her just last week and she still looks exactly the same. Now, since this ... at the very least unusual fact, is nothing new to my attention, I'll admit that when I first realized something was strange, about eight or so years ago, then I started paying more careful attention to this remarkable lady.

In a matter of just a few months, I discovered several extremely unusual little tidbits. Now, none of them alone is all that curious, but as you'll see, there are a rather substantial number of these 'discoveries' that I've made over the past few years and although not as frequently as was the case at first, the surprises still happen on occasion.

The first of these findings happened when one day I crossed paths with her at the local mall and because she was waiting for public transit, I offered her a ride home, since it was right on my way and there was a storm brewing. She accepted and we left the food court through doors on the western side of the facility and walked right into near gale force winds that were signaling that coming thunderstorm. Beeeep has long hair that is a combination of chestnut and red with near golden highlights. The stuff is straight as a ruler and always smoothly hanging down to below her collar, just as it was that day until the wind struck. My attention was drawn immediately to her as the wind lifted her locks and allowed me to see her left ear for what must have been the first time. I'm sure had it happened at some earlier time, I would have noticed and recalled that perfectly formed little ear. I say perfectly formed up to and including the little pointed top.

The only time I'd ever seen that ear shape that I could recall, was during the winter holidays when Santa's elves were represented in films with that very same ear design. So, before I could even control myself, I blurted out in exclamation.

"Hey, are you playing an elf or something?"

She blanched a pale shade before promptly turning a bright pink. Now I felt guilty for noticing.

"I'm sorry, I didn't mean to draw attention to something you're sensitive about."

After the walk to the car and getting in she pulled her opened fingers through the hair, recovering her left ear. Somehow, I just couldn't resist.

"Are both your ears that way?"

She turned those pale grey-green eyes to look me squarely in the face. I have an idea that it looks could have burned my skin, that stare would have been the delivery system. But without blinking or saying anything, she simply lifted the hair on the right side of her head, allowing me a good view of the right ear … which looked exactly like its mate.

"Is that something you had done with plastic surgery?"

Again, that silent glare.

"Okay, I'll guess not. I hope other kids don't tease you though."

"And why do you think they would do that?"

"I just remember when I was a school kid. Kids aren't always fair."

"Well, for one thing, none of them actually have seen them. It was a total accident that you did. I just wasn't thinking."

"So, you consciously try to keep that secret?"

She turned to look at me. We had just stopped for the traffic light going out of the mall.

There was a look in those eyes that said volumes, if only I knew how to translate it.

"Look Beeep, if you ever want to just talk to a completely non-judgmental adult, I'd be glad to listen."

That expression told me exactly what I wanted to actually hear. She did want to share with someone who might offer her advice or support or for whatever teenagers might be looking. It had been a long time since teenage for me. She turned to look out the window on her side of the car but then in a soft voice, almost as if she were talking to herself and didn't want me to hear what she was saying.

"How many years do you have?"

I should tell you at this point, I have been teaching college kids for the last sixteen years and I hold two doctorates. One is in anthropology and the other in history. And in all those years in college classrooms, twenty-one as a student and then another sixteen teaching, I had developed a pretty good set of diagnostic tools about things bothering students. More often it was nothing more than needing to talk to another party who is equipped with a compassionate ear. So, I made the offer.

"Look, sometimes it's … well just plain hard if not impossible to talk with a parent or sibling," she has an older brother, "or even a friend. It can be that you just need feedback from a non-involved adult. If you ever have that need, please don't hesitate to ask me."

Even though the answer was offered very softly and only a single word, I had high hopes.

"Sure." She said softly.

Some months later, in fact two *seasons* later, I had the opportunity to spend some time with Beeep. It was a party for her brother's graduation in late May. Being more than just a friend of the family and even a not-too-distant relation of her Mom's, got me an invite. It didn't hurt that I had written her brother Jacob a recommendation letter for college either. Who better to offer support than a college professor, right?

I would find out shortly that the party had two objectives. Being the end of May it was very nearly June 7th which was my brother's birthday. Beeep's mom is my brother's granddaughter. She was combining Jacob's graduation with a surprise birthday for Dave as well.

I was also shocked when I arrived at their home. I had heard a rumor that Beeeep was an artist of some quality. Walking into the entrance hall of her parent's house was more like a visit to a fairly high-end art gallery. As I was greeted and invited to come through the house, since the party was on the rear patio, I took my time to admire the dozen or so incredible paintings, watercolors, acrylic and oils. Most were of a moderate size in that twenty by twenty-four-inch range. But the one that really captured my attention was smaller, perhaps nine by twelve. The background was the most flesh like tone I'd ever seen on canvas. The center was a slightly stylized face of a tabby cat, in full yawn. My examination was interrupted by the sound of her voice. The surprise came from the facts that what she said was very soft as if only intended for my ears, and that she was only inches away and I'd not even realized I was not still alone.

"That's a painting of my tattoo. The inside of the mouth is my belly button."

What she had said took a minute to register. Was she even old enough for a tattoo?

"That tattoo is on your belly?"

One affirmative nod and she pulled up her tee-shirt from the front of her jeans to show me the real thing. And it was identical to the painting and in fact, the cat's open mouth was her belly button just as she had said. The tee-shirt dropped and she was gone, heading back toward the rear of the house. I followed.

Sure enough, the party was going strong. Her mom, Heather, was moving to and from the kitchen and her dad, Kirk, was at the gas grill doing burgers and such. At one end of the patio, there is a gazebo with screens around and the chairs in there were all occupied. I continued to follow Beeeep out into the back yard where a large tent has been set up with several tables. She was perhaps half dozen steps in front of me and I had a clear view of the stone path she followed. This is one of those things that I mentioned that I'd be telling you that you'll be saying that I'm making this up, but I'm just telling you what I saw.

As I walked along that stone path, with a perfectly manicured and verdant lawn surrounding it, as Beeeep passed little pale-yellow flowers, not dandelions but rather *Ranunculus* from Late Latin, or as we called them buttercups, seemed to just pop from the ground and when she took another step they disappeared. You know the flower I mean, at least if you grew up in the eastern US. Supposedly, if you pick the flower and hold it under a chin, if the chin reflects the yellow color, then that chin belongs to someone who loves butter. Now, while they do occur naturally in the east, they do not spontaneously appear and disappear just because someone passes by.

When I walked under the tent's edge and took a seat at the first open table, I quickly looked back along the path only to confirm that there were no flowers present. I contrived an excuse to request that Beeeep return to the house.

"Hey Beeeep, if you don't mind, when you go back to the house, would you bring me a bottle of water please? I should have gotten one on the way out here."

She looked at me with an impish grin and replied with a giggle in her voice.

"Why? Are you disbelieving your own eyes?"

And without hesitation, she ran over to the cooler on the patio. As I watched her along the path, both ways, nothing out of the ordinary happened. Apparently, my disappointment showed. So did her devilish smile.

"Don't worry, I'll do it again for you later."

"Wha …?"

This time the full giggle sprang from her face and her eyes sparkled with delight.

"Get you another bottle of water. Why, what did you think I meant?"

Chapter Two

So, you'll recall that I told you earlier that I'm a college professor and that I have two doctoral degrees. I have studied everything I could in a classroom environment that has to do with older cultures and societies including history, politics, economics, religion, mythology, which may well be the same in many cases, along with fears and suspicions related to witches, fairies, sprites and various sinister dark or even enlightened practitioners.

After my brief experience during that backyard party, I was unable to avoid reconsidering so much of what I'd read and to reevaluate my skepticism about the possibilities. First of all, the ears that reached a nearly pointed pinnacle are totally consistent with any and every detail I'd ever seen describing what can only be called fairy-like characteristics. The notion that fairies, were they to be an actual reality, are frequently associated in a positive and sharing symbiosis with Mother Nature and things like trees and flowers. So, to have flowers pop up in the midst of her passing … well, you know, if and that is a huge "*IF*" she were a fairy this might not be so hard to associate with her. Am I totally outside my mind? There is no way that fairies are real … is there?

One final decision I have reached is that my investigation is only beginning. I am going to sit down with her and just plain and simply ask her to explain what is going on. Sure, that'll work, won't it? There is something in me that just believes that if she is confronted that for whatever reason, she won't lie about what is the reality of her situation.

How many times when we are in a hurry to get to that task at the top of our list that we just can't seem to find the excuse to intrude into the very thing with which we are most eager to get involved? Well, this was not one of those times. As it turns out, the young lady who is the centerpiece of my investigation is an artist of some import. And likewise, I have the good fortune to be a supporter of the arts. When these two similarities caused our paths to cross the following Saturday at an outdoor art show at a local park, where she was showing several pieces and I was drafted to be a judge.

I made it a point to avoid talking with her at all while I was making my evaluation rounds along with two other fellow judges. I was very pleased when both my compatriots were as adamant as I about the very incredible nature of her work. She was awarded the first-place ribbon, and this even allowed me a legitimate excuse to stop by her space again afterward.

"So, Ms. 'best in the show' how much are you asking for the painting that won you the prize?"

"I was asking two hundred dollars for it, but since the end of the show is fast approaching and it did win best in the show, I'll reduce it to … ah, let's say two hundred *fifty* dollars!"

All this was offered with that sparkle of laughter and the devilish delight in her eyes.

"I'll take it!"

That stopped her dead in her tracks. The shock was more than obvious so I let the other shoe drop.

"I want to interview the artist included at that price too. Besides, I thought it was really underpriced when we walked through."

Now it was my turn to chuckle. In truth, the painting was easily worth double what I was paying for it, so I was pleased. My point was not lost on her either.

"Okay, the painting and an interview, but the interview has to be over lunch and you're buying. My choice!"

Another innocent giggle.

It should have come as no surprise that she would choose the Mexican restaurant that was only a few blocks away from the park. There was something about her that just struck me as … what … as international? Nah, that couldn't be.

After we were seated opposite each other in a two-person booth and had placed our orders, I decided to get right to the point.

"So, the pointy ears. Is that a birth defect or is there some other explanation?"

"What do you think? I can tell you there is nothing defective about my ears. They work just fine and they're cute don't you agree?"

"I didn't mean that they weren't attractive, but you have to admit, they are unusual. Right?"

"Not to me. Every time I've ever looked into a mirror, they've been just as they are today. That's the classic definition of normal."

"Normal for fairies maybe. Do you work for Santa?"

This caused her eyes to sparkle, and the burst of laughter caused other patrons to look toward our table.

"So, you think I'm one of Santa's elves? You do know that there is a huge difference between fairies and elves, right?"

"No ... I mean yes, I know that but ... well not necessarily. I'm just asking about your ears."

"I could be a garden gnome you know. Or maybe the tooth fairy or the guy with the pot of gold and the end of the rainbow. What do you think?"

"I don't know what I think. I just saw the ears and then at the party at your house ..."

"What did you see at the party?"

'I'm going to turn the tables here. What do you think I saw at the graduation party?"

"It could have been anything. Could have been the goldfish in the backyard fountain that my mom and I built or even the water changing colors with the music or flowers or something."

"I'm talking about the buttercups that popped up as you walked by and then just as quickly disappeared."

Suddenly there was a shy smile of her pretty face.

"Oh, you saw that?"

"So, I wasn't hallucinating?"

"I can't offer any diagnosis there."

"Oh no! You're not getting off that easily."

There was a look of genuine concentration suddenly replacing that shy smile and I could almost hear her gears turning. I wasn't sure if they were considering what she might admit or rather what lie might get her off the hook. And then she leaned in toward me and smiled easily.

"How old do you think I am?"

"Wha … I don't understand."

"It's a pretty straight forward question. How old am I?"

I considered that question before it occurred to me that I had known her for something like ten years and she had always been about the age she appeared to be now.

"I'd guess thirteen going on thirty-three."

She giggled at this.

"See, you've paid attention. Can I trust you to keep to yourself all that I'm about to share with you right now? And I'll even tell you why I'm willing to do it."

I nodded in the affirmative. But that wasn't enough. By an encouraging dip of her head, she let me know that she wanted me to *say* so. In an effort to be a wise ass, I told her.

"The saint's preserve us! I swear on me Celtic heritage to take these secrets to me grave."

I realized what I had said after it came out of my mouth. Okay, I thought, I'm going round the bend for sure. But the radiance that little speech generated around her face shocked me more than what I'd said.

"I knew it was you! I knew it had to be because the time has passed, and I have things to do."

"What the hell are you talking about now?"

"I'll explain all of it to you. Just be patient and understand that you are not going to believe most of what I tell you even though inside you will *feel* that it is true because your inner self will know that it's true."

Over the following hour, she relayed a tale to me, the sorts of which I'd never even imagined in my wildest fantasies. Keep in mind that, as I sort of confessed in my pledge to her, I am, of Celtic descent and being a Scotsman and known to partake of the highlands nectar as often as possible, resulting in all sorts of imaginings.

What did she share with me you might ask? Again, keep your mind as open as is humanely possible. Everything I will repeat here for your consideration is exactly what she told me of. She was so simplistic and straight forward as she revealed item after item. I am left with the distinct feeling that it is all true, even if it is out of the realm of normal.

Beeep first informed me that she is for all practical purposes, ageless. When I asked what that specifically meant, she responded with the brief statement that she is without any specific age. She explained that she appears to be of the age that people expect when they see her. When it was obvious to her that I didn't understand what that meant, she added that she was the reincarnation of an Irish Celtic girl named Brigid. That girl was born in 451 A.D. in Dundalk, County Kildare, Ireland. She was the patron of poor farm people, especially farm children and midwives.

Now that I had so much information, I was heading to do what I do best, research. There had been any number of things she told me that I could either verify or dismiss. My work was certainly cut out for me for the next few days.

Little did I realize that a few days would not be required. Within minutes of beginning my search, I was slammed with a realization that the girl she had described was a Catholic saint. Saint Brigid was born in County Kildare, Ireland in 451and was the patron saint of babies, brewers, *farmers* and more.

Brigid, the Celtic goddess of fire, is known to love and support and encourage poetry, healing, childbirth, was born at the exact moment of daybreak, and as legend reports, Brigid rose into the sky at exactly sunrise, with the rays like fire beaming from her head. The tales of Saint Brigid do share many things that might be interpreted as similar.

When we compare the myths of the goddess Brigid with those legends of Saint Bridgit, we find that they are just as super-natural. Brigid, either as the Goddess or the Saint and whether or not either was actually a mortal woman remains a reasonable question.

What is known is that Saint Bridgit was the human daughter of a family in February, 521 in County Kildare, Ireland. The goddess on the other hand, upon an undocumented birth was fed milk from a sacred cow from the Otherworld.

One cherished tale of Saint Bridgit is that wherever she might walk, small flowers and shamrocks will appear. This was a phenomenon I had already witnessed first-hand.

It is said that Goddess Bridgit as a sun goddess brought her gifts of light (knowledge), inspiration, and the vital and healing energy of the sun.

Our Bridgette without question then, is at the very least, a follower of Saint Bridgit. Now the project she had wanted my help with made perfect sense.

Chapter Three

The first major conclusion I reached with my research, besides analyzing any number of details, was that I now had a new purpose in life and the responsibilities that went along with that were considerable. The first and most important thing at the moment was to locate a place from which we could operate. I guess at this point we'll call it a studio. You know, a kind of club house for artists, a home base by whatever choice I could make.

The perfect place hit me like a ton of bricks dropped from a very high altitude. You see, I own some commercial rental properties and one of those is an old building on the corner of Main and Thirteenth Streets where back around the late nineteenth century there was a company that made buggies and wagons and other horse drawn conveyances. It was once upon a time the home offices and factory for Piano-Box Buggy Works.

After the company went belly up in 1924, the building sat idle for many years until in 1950 the local Ford dealer moved their used car department into the facility. Within another twenty years, with downtowns being all but deserted for the suburbs, the building once again became a sore on the storefront street.

Depending upon your perspective, I was either the unlucky or lucky person to have nearly stolen the place when it sold at auction in the early eighties. I had rented it to a parts company for a warehouse and then even that company decided to get out of the city and closer to where business might be found.

Now I just covered expenses by letting a friend who restores classic cars pay those related costs like taxes, insurance, and utilities in exchange for using the ground floor space. When I called him to let him know that I needed to use some of the second-floor space myself, he was agreeable without hesitation.

And that is how it became the badly needed 'clubhouse' or 'studio' for Beeeep and me. Now I should explain that we needed a space to meet on a regular basis for logistics and debriefing. Jeez that sounds like we're some sort of spy network or professional hit squad. Well, rest assured we are neither.

Upon her first visit, Beeeep immediately looked around the dusty old second floor room and announced.

"The New Caledonia Exchange! It's perfect, well it will be with some paint and cleaning."

This was punctuated by her bubbling giggle and a dance that swirled her around, dragging her right-hand fingertips across window ledges and the few pieces of old furniture, as if she were offering some sort of blessing. Small funnels of dust swirled in the streaks of sunlight coming through the dirty windows.

Over the next few days, I called in contractors and cleaners. The building, as I mentioned, is on the corner of Main and Thirteenth Streets, runs through the block to Water Street and is about two blocks from the river. Main runs east and west and Thirteenth spans north to south. On the southeast front of the building, our exchange occupies half the width facing Main which is about thirty feet and the length of it runs along thirteenth Street for about a hundred feet to the corner of Water Street. The front or south, and east-side walls are windowed from about two feet above the floor to about two feet from the overhead which is exposed joists and the flooring above. You've seen the old factory windows that have metal frames with panes that are twelve by twelve inches. Each section is ten rows of glass high and twelve rows wide. The center section of the window which is six panes tall and 8 panes wide and center hinged on a rod which allows the window to be tilted opened.

During the work being done, all the windows were cleaned, the frames painted and restored to working order. I had sheetrock installed on all the walls except the front and side walls which are made of the thick brick that is also the exterior of the building. At Beeeep's request, the brick was painted with a dark blue gloss enamel and the drywall was painted in a much lighter shade of blue/grey. The trim, along with the window frames was done in black.

The job was completed with a coat of black floor and deck on the random width oak floorboards. After that final painting was done, the toilet, shower stall and sink were set in the little room at the rear which we had created for that purpose.

Using the water and drain connected for the little bath, I decided to add a small kitchenette on the outside wall of the bath. In a wall of manufactured cabinets, we have a stainless sink, a sixty-inch counter with cabinets above and a refrigerator, a narrow gas range and small round café table with four chairs.

I called Beeeep to ask if she'd like to see the finished product. Within twenty minutes, she was coming up the stairs from our rear entrance off Water Street. There was a strange sound following her, so I went to investigate.

From the top of the stairs, I could see that there was some sort of long object or perhaps a dead body wrapped in a blanket that was attached to something that looked like a backpack which was hanging on her by shoulder straps. She was slowly taking one up step at a time owing to the load. I quickly slipped by her and grasped the lower end of what turned out to be a heavy roll and assisted her up to our space.

She was extremely proud of herself when she used a small pocket-knife to slit the binder's twine that held the bundle rolled tightly. In moments she pulled and unfurled a still beautiful if somewhat moth bitten Persian carpet in shades of gold, red and navy blue. Much of the fringe at either end was missing, but as she straightened it on the open floor, I saw the usefulness of it.

"I can't believe the deal I got on this beautiful old rug. One of our neighbors had a yard sale last Saturday and I waited until it was about over and offered her ten dollars for the rug and she took it! It's twelve by eighteen."

"Does it fly or anything like that?"

Okay, I'll admit I was being a smartass, but given what I already knew about this young lady, it might be forgiven. Of course, she took the comment as a challenge and with that impish expression on her face she responded in kind.

"I don't know. Move back a bit and let's see what she can do."

For almost a minute I stood there actually expecting something to happen. I guess it did happen too. She burst out laughing.

After a few minutes of awkward silence, I took a seat at one of the two matching oak swivel desk chairs I'd gotten from a used furniture store down the street. Without hesitation, she took a seat in the other and turned to address me.

"Do you have a lucky number? Mine is nine. Did you know that every multiple of nine adds up to another nine?

"Like, for example the early numbers like eighteen and twenty-seven and eighty-one are pretty obvious one plus eight or eighteen and the two and seven of twenty-seven and the eight and one of eighty-one all add up to nine again.

"But even with bigger numbers like nine times twenty-seven is two hundred forty-three and the two plus four plus three is nine again. Even the really big numbers like Forty-one hundred fifty-nine times nine equals thirty-seven thousand four hundred thirty-one and all that added together equals eighteen and that one and eight added equal nine.

"And then huge numbers like twenty-one thousand six hundred fifty-eight times nine is one hundred ninety-four thousand nine hundred twenty-two and adding those digits together equals twenty-seven and the two and seven added together equals nine all over again.

"See, nine is really a magical number that stays in every permutation of itself. It never leaves its relatives alone. See?"

"You know Beeeep, sometimes you amaze me and then sometimes you totally amaze me."

She giggled, delighted with herself apparently then got back down to business.

"We're going to need some office supplies. Not much but maybe some pens and legal pads for notes and lists."

I pulled open the top right-hand drawer of the desk in front of me, removed a pad of paper and a jell pen passing both to her. She needed no further invitation and began scribbling a shopping list for whatever we would need. At some point I realized that while the space was already a sunk cost, I'd spent about three thousand dollars on the recent improvements and keep in mind that college professors don't make tons of money. So, I made a suggestion.

"Be gentle on my wallet please."

She stopped mid-whatever she was writing and looked me dead in the eye. She made no comment while she was contemplating my request. But suddenly her eyes brightened.

"Do you know who Alanna Michel was?"

I'd not heard the name since I was a child and would sit on my grandfather's knee and hear his tales of old Scotland. Alanna was his favorite sibling, his baby sister who was about ten or twelve years his junior.

When the family relocated to the United States in 1928, just a year before the stock market crash on Black Monday, my grandfather was an eighteen-year-old and his baby sister was only seven with two remaining brothers and one sister between them. These five children were all that remained of the original eleven and were being brought to America for a chance at a better life. The two brothers would both die in WWII serving their new country. The sister, closest in age to Warwick would precede him by several years, having never married.

"Yes. She was my grandfather's baby sister. Why?"

She giggled brightly and replied.

"Well, you see, they had the same parents and that's why she was your grandfather's sister. Don't you have like two PhD's?"

"You know that's not what I meant. I meant why did you bring her up?"

"Well *now* I understand your question."

"And are you going to share the answer with me?"

"Well, I need to ask you something first."

"Okay."

"Did she have any other heirs?"

"I know she didn't have any children because she had something like Scarlett Fever as a kid and the doctors thought that was why she couldn't have kids. Again, why?"

"Let me see if I can explain this to you. Your grandfather and his family moved from Scotland to the US. There were how many kids? Five, right? Your grandfather had your dad and your dad had you. Now your grandfather's two brothers died in World War Two, with no kids, right?"

I nodded in the affirmative and tried to look impatient so she would hurry along.

"His other sister who was an elementary school teacher and died before your grandfather did. And she didn't have any kids?"

Another nod showed my agreement with her analysis so far.

"That means that you are the only member of your family in this generation, correct?"

I considered that for a few seconds and while I knew that she was correct. I would have to later question just how she knew all this stuff.

"Yes, you are correct. None of grandfather's other kids had any kids and I'm an only child as well, so I guess I am all that remains of that entire family of seven that immigrated in 1928. So, what does all that mean?"

"It means that you are her only heir. She died two days ago and had no will. I think the term is intestate. By California law, that means that all her property of value passes to the nearest living relative. But you're going to have to make a claim. In fact, you might want to start by contacting the authorities there and making final arrangements for her?"

"How do you know all this stuff?"

The sheepish smile was cute but wasn't telling me anything. I expressed my frustration with a broad shoulder shrug and elevating my arms in a pleading gesture, palms open and upward.

"I ... well, I just know stuff. It sorta ... well it comes to me when I need it. You know, it's sort of like some special ... energy is as good a description as anything."

I considered that for half a minute before the next question jumped up.

"So, this energy ... is it always ... like fully charged?"

"Oh no! It only happens ... well sometimes and then the energy sort of drops, you know like a battery that charges and then discharges and has to recharge again."

"And does it, as you said, recharge on its own?"

She chuckled, shaking her head as if amazed at the stupidity of my question.

"Of course, it does. I don't have to like be plugged in or something."

The look on her face suddenly changed substantially and I realized that she wanted to say something else about it but had thought better of it. Needless to say, I wanted her to say whatever it was that she had on her mind, so I prodded.

"C'mon, what were you going to say? There's something else isn't there?"

This time I got a sheepish nod of her head and her eyes looked down at her feet and she added in a soft voice.

"There is a quick way to recharge me."

"What's that?"

"Well, if you kiss the bottoms of each toe on my left foot …"

I was totally not expecting that sort of situation. Now what?

"Well, take off your left shoe."

I really had no idea what I was planning to do next, but I should have known better by now.

She burst into a peal of giggles, bending over with both her hands on her stomach. When she could finally catch a breath, she looked up at me with tears in her eyes and mirth on her face.

"You were really going to kiss my toes! Didn't you know I was jerking your chain?"

And such was the beginning of our partnership. I was leaning away from the whole fairy notion and becoming more inclined to think some sort of impish wood nymph.

I now was left with other questions, and I would eventually realize that many more questions would come with each answer I was able to discern or to squeeze from Beeep. It would simply become a fact of life.

"Now you can explain our need to involve my late Great Aunt Alanna?"

Again, the sheepish look of innocence that I was growing far too accustomed to seeing. I raised my shoulders in a questioning shrug.

"Well… you see the project is going to have some requirements that will be far more expensive than this building and three thousand dollars of work and office supplies."

"Like what?"

She flipped open her little vinyl brief and pulled out a sheet of lined yellow paper from a legal pad.

"I just happen to have a list here with me. We are going to need a building to prepare as a residence. Then another building, maybe an old factory building where we can create a hydroponic farm. Then it will need renovations that will include converting it to solar power and taking water from the river for irrigation.

"We're going to create the N-gener-8 Agronomics Foundation. This name is based on the meanings of a couple words: **"Ngener8"** **(*Ingenerate*)** – is natural, organic; to engender, produce as in inborn, innate; then "***Agronomics***" **(agronomy)** is the science of production of field crops.

I have already accepted the fact that I only understand half or less of what comes from Beeep.

She has an infinite capacity to say things that do not fall anywhere along the normal spectrum.

"Wait… wait, are we going into some sort of business?"

Her expression went from confident to disbelief in 4 seconds.

"No, not a business. It is a charity endeavor. I thought you already understood."

"I thought this studio was what you wanted. What are the others you mentioned? A residence? For whom? And a factory building to be a farm? I got lost there somewhere. Are we're gonna buy those?"

"Well yeah. That's why we need you inheritance."

"Maybe, you could start at the beginning and give me the total plan, including everything we might need. Could you do that?"

She nodded her head and smiled.

"Yes, I can do that. My idea, no, it's more a goal and a plan to accomplish that goal. I want to help homeless and near homeless people by providing them a place to live, a residential facility. Then I want to give them a purpose, a self-image with gainful employment by teaching them to be farmers. We raise organic vegetables using all-natural processes. We sell the high-end vegetables to regional distributors, markets, and restaurants. We use that money to maintain the entire operation."

"You're saying that in addition to this place, we need to buy two more buildings?"

Bridgette nodded vigorously in the affirmative.

"Yeah! And we're gonna need more help, probably a few trucks, a bus, equipment, renovations to convert one building to a residence hall and one to an indoor farm."

"Have you worked out a projected budget? I mean any idea how much all this will cost?"

"No, but I can. I'll need to consult with a couple friends. Also, we are going to need help in the areas of professional drivers, agricultural work, residential services, maintenance, repairs, construction/renovation and other stuff, I'm sure.

"But don't worry. I'll find whatever we need when we need it. That's what I'm good at!"

Chapter Four

I had only a vague idea of where Great Aunt Alanna's home was. I remember that she had married a Greek immigrant and that they had a vineyard of something. I started my internet research with New York and California. Beeeep had also mentioned California inheritance laws. Even though I still had no freaking idea how she knew stuff, I had no other real option as a starting point. At least I was dealing with an unusual name.

I did a people search online that was listed as "free" which of course meant nothing of the sort. Sure, these sites offer free search, but they don't let you see the info returned on the search until you pay the lying bastards. Still, for a couple of bucks, I quickly discovered some incredible information about my aunt Alanna Lily Blair Michel. Alanna lived for seventy years in the city of Salinas, California. Her husband Arron Michel who was a vintner's son followed the family business with an ever so slight bent to suit his own road.

In 1947, shortly after moving to Salinas, he opened a company where he created two labels of whiskey. The first was an American single malt and the second an American blended whiskey. His company was Saint Michel Distillery and the brands he manufactured, using all American ingredients and mountain water were Angels Mist and Alanna Blended Whiskey. And his crazy idea was to age whiskey in old used wine barrels.

In 1999, at the age of eighty Arron had retired and sold his company to a conglomerate of whiskey makers for a substantial sum which he had, with the assistance of the company lawyers, invested in several places including a tidy sum of stock in the company that had acquired his and in real estate and other things. These details were not readily available online.

Arron had passed in 2006 leaving his entire estate to his widow Alanna. The fortune was large at that time. One of the things I was able to glean was that the firm of Albosta, Dea and Campbell had handled the estate settlement a decade ago.

Another three minutes and I'd found that firm located in Orange County and secured contact information.

My first task the following day after my classes were over was to make a phone call to the attorney in Orange County.

"Albosta associates, how may I help you?"

"Good morning. My name is Warwick Blair. I understand that your firm handled the estate of the late Arron Michel of Salinas. That was back in 2006. Might I speak with the attorney who handled that please?"

"Might I inquire as to the nature of your call?"

"Yes. Arron Michel was married to my great aunt, Alanna Blair Michel. She has recently passed, and I was only made aware of it yesterday. I am her only remaining family member and I'd like to make final arrangements for her. I am going to need assistance with finding out where she is and her current status as well as what is necessary to prove my relationship."

"Yes sir, mister Blair, please hold."

Seconds later a very pleasant female answered.

"Mister Blair, I'm Claire Campbell. How can I assist you?"

I went through the entire back story including that there was no other family, and I didn't actually know the current status of anything, including where my great aunt was. The attorney took my contact information and what details I had regarding my great aunt, her late husband, and the last address for their home in Salinas. She agreed to get back to me as quickly as she had an update. She further told me all that would be required to document my relationship with the deceased.

My next agenda item was to create a list of where I might locate each document I would need to verify my relationship with my late great aunt. Fortunately, my training in anthropology had nearly forced me into doing an ancestral research paper in graduate school. From that investigation, I had research support of the immigration of my grandparents along with my father and the four siblings who were with the family at the time. I had saved copies of their birth certificates as well as death announcements and marriage licenses and other pertinent data.

I also had copies of published obituaries which showed repeated documentation of all relatives in each case.

This was one day that I was pleased to have made the decision to avoid any summer school classes at the college. Normally, I would teach both sessions each summer owing to the fact that I earned an added ten percent of my annual salary for each of those sessions and the money was handy. Not to mention, what else would I be doing with that time anyway?

I was surprised to find my 'partner' already at the center when I arrive at eleven thirty the following morning. And more than just being present, she was in a hurry to do things.

"I was just beginning to wonder when you'd get here."

"I didn't know we had a work schedule already. I've been trying to get other stuff done. Besides, I haven't heard anything from the attorney in California yet and we are going to need some money."

There was a smile that approached being a smirk on her face as she responded.

"I suspect that your phone will ring shortly and the news you get will solve any idea of a problem with money. Be patient."

That was a first. Being told to be patient by a thirteen or fourteen or even an eighteen-year-old was totally unheard of. Then it occurred to me that very thing was something I should know.

"By the way, how old are you?"

The question came from somewhere deep in my sub-conscious. I had not thought about it in days and suddenly it was on my lips and the first realization I had of its arrival was when I heard it come out. Bridgette had that effect on me.

"Is chronology all that important? I mean, really? You've heard that God made the world in six days and rested on the seventh, yes?"

I nodded in agreement, curious where this might be headed.

"Well, since He hasn't done anything for thousands of years, while resting, and this being that seventh day, that the scientists are more than likely correct saying that those first six days may have been millions of Earth years long. So, if I were to say that I am ... oh, what do you like? Sixteen or eighteen or maybe even twenty, that might be a lot longer than you think, right? I mean if my years are, say, twenty of yours. See what I mean."

Before I could even consider what she had said, my phone rang. When I looked at the screen and saw that the caller ID was for the law firm in Orange, California.

"Hello, this is Wick Blaire."

"Mister Blaire, this is Claire Campbell. I have gotten together the information you wanted. Some of it is good and some is exceptionally good but with a bit of frustration."

"Excellent. Let me just get a pad of paper and a pen to make notes."

"Actually, it might be better if I just email you a digital copy of this collection of data. If I could get an email address, I will have my assistant get it to you in a few minutes. Then just call me with questions. I should say though that your aunt has left a comprehensive will which I will also forward to you. It seems that she was aware that you were the only remaining heir and addressed that as well as making her own final arrangements which have already been completed."

I shared my private email address and thanked her for her assistance. By the time I had booted up my laptop, the email was already present. It had several attachments. I mumbled a comment to myself about wishing we had a printer at the center and was shocked when I received a reply.

"You mean like this one?"

Beeep did her best pretty girl game show helper imitation, indicating a wireless laser printer which she had apparently installed prior to my arrival this morning and showed me that charming grin with a flutter of eyelashes.

As I opened the attachments one by one, I sent them to the printer which she has also added to our little wireless local network. Bridget turned and added paper to the feeder as the multiple pages began to come through. Within several minutes there was a half-inch stack of printed pages on the corner of my desk.

My first selection was the will. As I leaned back in my desk chair, I saw the standard legalese that included being of sound mind and body, etc. The first statements had to do with her own final arrangements. She had apparently made all those plans and made the payments in advance shortly after the passing of her husband in 2006. This section was the majority of all the will except for a single statement that all the real estate, investments, monies, and other properties having any monetary value shall be set into a closed trust until her remaining sole heir is located at which time that trust will pass fully to him. She identified him only as the only child of her nephew William Cottaway Blair and Grandson of her brother Warwick Cottaway Blair. This last generation son was, according to the beliefs of Alanna, one Warwick Cottaway Blair II.

The second page had several signatures which were witnessed and sealed by a notary in 2006. I realized at that point my only requirement was to prove that I am, in fact, that Warwick Cottaway Blair II.

Immediately following was a page that had even solved that problem for me. There was a codicil dated in June 2007 that identified me specifically by describing where I had attended college and that I was employed at the university as a professor.

As I slumped back a bit in the desk chair, I realized that Beeeep wasn't at her desk any longer, but I also heard at the same time the sounds of voices on the stairs. Within moments Beeeep came into the office and was followed by an elderly gentleman of about six feet and what thinning hair that remained was snow white. He had a very benign expression and had nearly the look of clergy. What was she up to now I wondered?

"Wick, this is an old friend of mine. His name is Uncle Ray. You may be familiar with the Middle Eastern beliefs in the God of sun, and often air and creativity later, who was known as Rae or Rhea."

That was pretty much her full explanation. I was left wondering if I was to believe that this man she had just brought in was some sort of elderly God from the Sahara. Still, I refused to be rude, so I rose and offered my hand to him. When he clasped my right hand, the heat that came from him was surprising and intense.

I offered him a seat in one of my side chairs which he accepted with a nod of his head.

"What can we do for you Uncle Ray?"

His smile was completely benevolent, and I'd swear created additional light in the room.

"Au contraire, mon ami. I am here to help you with your efforts."

I looked up at Beeeep with what I am sure was a questioning look. She grinned and responded.

"Uncle Ray has worked with me in the past on other projects. He wants to help so I figured more hands make light work. No pun intended Uncle Ray."

And that delighted giggle that she so often employed was there instantly. She then sat down and looked at me expectantly.

"So, the email that you printed. Good news I'm going to assume? Do you want to share the details?"

How does she just immediately know these things? That was one thing I intended to get to the bottom of and it was going to be soon or else.

"As a matter of fact, I had just finished reading the will itself but not the attachments. The will names me as sole heir and reasonably identifies me. I am to receive whatever she left. I just don't know yet what that might be."

"Then the best part is yet to come!"

She was excited, almost like a child waiting for a parent to open the gift from her on Christmas morning.

"Perhaps. But equally likely, I may owe her final expenses."

"Wick! Really? I mean, she and her husband owned a very successful company that made whiskey and had vineyards and more. She was at the very least a multi-millionaire. Use your noggin for once."

She shook her hand toward me in a get busy gesture, so I decided to look at the estate inventory list. I started to browse through the remaining pages. There were several sheets of account descriptions that included words like annuity, trust, development, assets and so on. I regretted for the first time not taking any business courses in college. But as if my eyes had been directed toward it, I saw that each page had in the lower right corner a 'page total' for what was listed there. So, I quickly flipped through the nearly twenty pages until I saw one of those that was indicated as the 'estate total value'. My mind instantly went totally numb. Was I reading this correctly? How could I be? The number had far too many digits. There was a dollar sign followed by numbers in this order, 2,087,506,880.00. I could not speak. Was I right in thinking that this amount was over two *billion* dollars? I must be mistaken, or something was wrong in my interpretation.

"What? What?"

Obviously, she had been watching me for some reaction and when my reaction was to go numb and silent, she must have assumed that something awful had happened. I looked up at her and those gorgeous pale eyes were opened to a full roundness I had not seen more than two or three times ever. Rather than reply, I just handed her the sheet I had been staring at for however long I'd been semi-comatose. She did not hesitate in snatching it away and examining what was printed there. Then with a single burst of laughter or excitement she screeched.

"Holy billions batman! No money worries now!"

"So, I did read it correctly then?"

"What do you mean? You're getting more than two billion dollars."

"Well, I'm sure there will be inheritance taxes and legal fees and other stuff about which

I'm not aware. That will probably take most of it, right?"

"No way! You have a lawyer, haven't you? Call him and ask."

I considered that for a minute and then it occurred to me that the lawyer who would be most familiar with this was the one from whom I had gotten it. Checking the clock to confirm the time in Orange County California. She should be in her office now. I grabbed my cell phone and checked the contacts to which I had added the number of the law firm when I first called. I selected it and hit the dial button.

"Good morning, Albosta, Dea and Campbell, how may I direct your call?"

"Hello, this is Doctor Warwick Blair. I talked with Ms. Campbell a couple of times over the past couple of days and she has sent me a package. She said that if there were questions to give her a call. Is she in and available?"

Moments later the attorney was on the line.

"It's doctor, is it? Medical or academic?"

"Academic."

"I apologize for missing that before. My brother and sister-in-law are both academic doctors, so I understand the correct usage. What questions do you have then Doctor Blair?"

"Well, I'm a bit embarrassed to admit, I'm not particularly informed in wills and inheritances and the related taxes, fees and legal costs associated with them."

"The paperwork I forwarded to you is the final inventory of the estate. All filing fees, legal fees, your aunt's final expenses and inheritance taxes have been paid. Your report is exactly what you will receive at distribution. While we are on that topic, might I suggest that it would be expeditious for you to come to California for that distribution. That will allow you to present documentation that you are, in fact, the great nephew as well as the opportunity to see the real estate and to convert the accounts. The corporate office for Wells Fargo is in San Francisco. If you create an account at your local Wells Fargo Bank, then it will be a simple matter of moving from your Aunt's accounts to your own while you are here. That will avoid any added bank transfer fees."

"What exactly should I bring with me as proof of who I am?"

"Actually, that's pretty simple. Bring your birth certificate as well as a photo ID that has the same name on it. You might want to include your social security card and if you have documentation of the demise of your father and perhaps your paternal grandfather just to be on the safe side should there be questions. A published obituary for your father and grandfather will certainly be adequate. You probably will not need all that unless some question comes up. Then it will save you time and avoid any further legal action or another trip out here for that."

"Thank you. Now, should we set an appointment for my trip out?"

"Why don't you just evaluate your schedule as to when it would work best for you. Then once you book your flight, and incidentally, it would be best if you flew into LAX, contact me and I'll make time based on your schedule."

Chapter Five

    I shared the latest information with my now two office mates and then proceeded to make airline reservations, followed by arranging a hotel and rental car in Los Angeles.

    Beeeep was deep in conversation with Uncle Ray while I made short work of putting together my trip. I had until Tuesday, and today was Friday. When I finally addressed them and shared my findings and plans, neither of them even reacted to the mammoth amount of money I was to inherit. I had the distinct impression that they had both already known before I had found out. I really need to get over thinking that way. I mean, there's no way, right?

"So, I am going to need to go buy one of those portable navigation things or something of that sort so when I get to the airport in Los Angeles, I'll be able to find Orange County. And I'll need to go by the news office and get copies of the obits for Dad and Grandpapa. What do you have planned?"

This last question was addressed directly to my erstwhile sole partner. At this point I was pretty sure that Uncle Ray was going to be a keeper. She didn't hesitate.

"We're going to look at a school building out on Riverview Boulevard. It was built in 1921 and has about thirty-eight thousand square feet, it is zoned for multiple occupancy plus it has almost three acres around it and is for sale by the city because it isn't used any more. They're asking two hundred eighty-five thousand dollars for it. That's only seven and a half dollars a square foot. You can't build the outside walls for that!"

I was once again stopped in my tracks. Though I did consciously consider not saying anything since I was sure I still wouldn't know even if she told me.

"How in the world did you know all that?"

It was more an exclamation than a question, but she offered an answer of sorts, none-the-less.

"I read a lot."

"And you're going to look at it … why?"

"Because it will make a perfect residential space for homeless people. Duh!"

And with that total explanation, NOT, she and her Uncle Ray were bouncing down the stairs. I hoped that at some point, I'd catch up. I mean, I do have two PhD's. Count 'em. I'm reasonably intelligent.

Fortunately, I had enough smarts to call the news office before making the trip out there for the obits. They informed me that all that information was available at the public library in a digital format which could generate copies for about a nickel each page.

On the way to the library, my curiosity got the better of me, so I decided to drive out Riverview Blvd. to take a look at the school building that Beeeep found so exciting. It was a yellow brick structure dating from 1921. Built in an 'H' shape with the crossbar being the center and front façade with wings on either end, it was three stories and if I recalled correctly housed sixteen classrooms as well as offices, library, cafeteria, auditorium, and gymnasium.

There was an eight by four-foot sign on what appeared to be a sheet of white painted plywood. It announced to all the passersby that it was indeed for sale and zoned R-5 meaning fairly high-density multiple occupancy. This information meant the property could be converted to condos, apartments, or lofts in the popular vernacular.

The building was already plumbed for multiple rest rooms as well as a full cafeteria. The location was good too for its access to public transportation. My reaction was mostly one of curiosity. Now I wanted to see the interior with some idea of what my 'partner' had in mind as to usage.

With some mental images about what might be, I headed off to the public library. Our city, like many at this time in history, had experienced the development of shopping centers in the early 1960s which were then replaced by malls in the eighties. At one such location our city management had gotten a good deal on a former department store and converted the space to a central public library.

Upon arrival there I was offered assistance in locating the items I desired and even had help making the copies of the documents after I located them. Armed with this portion of the documentation I needed, I headed home to prepare for my trip.

For whatever reason, my mind had the distinct impression that I was being summoned as I let my shoulders sag with the relief of having all that I needed to prove I am who I believe I am. But the urge to stop by our studio was more than just an idea and since I was going to be gone a few days next week, I figured what the hey.

I did not have any idea what I expected to find when I arrived. If I'd actually considered it, I suppose I should have been surprised that Beeeep and Uncle Ray were both there and engaged in an animated discussion about possibilities and potentials. From what I caught as I entered the office, they were talking about jobs training and farming and food and projects to support the residents. To minimize my situation, you might just say, I was totally confused.

The did stop talking and both looked up to me as it I had all the answers just as I walked in.

"What …"

Uncle Ray took the lead without any competition.

"We're discussing ways for our future residents to feel a part of their own salvage and support. While giving them a roof over their heads is important, it is only part of the process."

Still the word my mind came up with was flabbergasted.

"Okay, I'm just going to quit acting like I know what's going on here. So, will someone tell me … please?"

Uncle Ray looked at our pretty little partner in crime or at least, his partner in secrecy, shook his head and with a questioning glance turned the floor over to Beep.

This was not the first time I had seen that sheepish look of innocence and I suspected that it would not be the last, but she squared her shoulders and addressed the issue directly to me.

"This ... "

She waved her hand around to indicate our club house.

"... what we have started here, is something that Uncle Ray and I have done before. Our motivation is to help others who are less fortunate. And the others I mean are people or animals or ... well whatever or whomever needs helping.

"Our present focus is trying to help homeless people get a place to spend cold and rainy nights under a roof with heat and even a clean toilet and a few meals to keep them going.

"The school building, we looked at today has eighteen classrooms which if used correctly is enough space for seventy-two residential rooms. The rooms are roughly twenty by forty feet. If they are divided into little suites, each classroom might become four suites of about ten by twenty feet less the thickness of walls. Say each suite would two rooms of nine and a half by eight feet, with a door into the corridor and a window in the bedroom. A little sitting and study area divided from the bedroom by a block set aside as a closet and storage compartment of about six by four feet. We can build in a platform bed so it would only need a mattress and in the sitting area, a built- in sofa and a desk. Perfect housing for a single person."

That light coming on in the brain is really something that does happen. In that instant, not only did I realize what she had been planning all along, but I had several ideas toward that same goal.

"So, we buy the school building and convert it to a homeless shelter? The school has toilets, showers, rooms, even a library if we choose to stock it and there is office space for those workers who will be employed as our support staff. And the cafeteria and the auditorium can feed them and be used for entertainment and training."

"Yes! And more. We have other ideas. To make money to pay for operations of the place.

"There is a fairly good-sized parking lot behind the building and it's right next to what was a playground. We repave all that and add in a car wash and create a contract with the city to keep the police and staff cars and trucks clean in exchange for a reduced cost and a break on the taxes, and the folks living in the place can run the car wash."

I considered all this for a few moments before another thunder cloud with bolts of light struck me in the head.

"Let's take it one or two steps further. Suppose that down along the river, we buy one of those old, deserted factory buildings. We renovate that to become a hydroponic farm. We train our residents to be farmers and packers and shippers and whatever else we need to make it work.

"This thing might become self-sustaining after a bit."

When I stopped and looked at Beeep, I don't know what I expected to see, but I knew without a doubt that she had not only embraced my idea but perhaps had gone onto the next step or two.

"Yes! And we use solar power and water from the river, but only to grow *organic* vegetables on the old factory floors. We can use them to feed our residents as well as selling them at local supermarkets. We need to have a name that represents all of this."

It was no surprise that Uncle Ray joined in at that point. He was, after all, the scientist and probably a Ph.D. as well.

"I have the perfect thought there. How does the name Ingenerate Agronomics sound? Quite simply ingenerate means native or natural or organic and the science of soil and agriculture is known as agronomy. Our employees are native to the area, and they will be doing soil management and farming. The name covers it all."

I must confess the name sounded perfect but as I wrote it on the pad of paper in front of me, I saw something that would make it look more contemporary. I turned the pad so I could write the letters larger then showed it to my two cohorts.

"How about this? And it will always be printed in bold green on whatever it appears.

Ingenerate basically means innate or to bring about generation. Natural. And, whenever it is printed, either on stationary, business cards or even signs it should be in a bright spring-like green."

The N-gener-8 Agronomics Foundation

The vote was unanimous. We had our name at that moment, almost as if by fluke. Add one more thing to my to do list. Verify availability of the name and create a not-for -profit corporation.

"Now, while I'm on my trip to California, can you two work on a business organization that can handle all of the stuff that will be needed? You know, like staffing to run the entire process. We will need a buildings and grounds maintenance department, a person in charge of training, counseling, sales and procurement, and most importantly a human resources group that includes someone with a social services background."

I realized that Bridgette was staring into some void, and she was perfectly quiet.

"Bridge, is there something else that you see or feel a need to add or comment upon?"

"You're getting better at this whole mind-reading thing!

Followed by her patented little giggle.

"And this time you for sure, got it right! I have a really good friend who is totally into dogs. She has a pet sitting service and she supports training for service dogs too. Her business is called Petrie's Pooch Services. She and I thought it would be very helpful to have service dogs available for residents of our programs.

"She even offered to provide the dogs, train them and then train residents so they can work together.

"And since so many homeless need to be loved and a happy dog will love anyone who is good to them. It would be a great thing that will help people and animals at the same time.

"Bridgette, that is a brilliant idea! When you think about this, then not only can we help homeless people, we also can help address homelessness for stray dogs!"

"Yeah, and very few people have any idea about the number of dogs become homeless in an average year. Last year about six hundred seventy thousand dogs are euthanized of the three million plus that enter animal shelters after being abandoned. And that number only represents the ones lucky enough to get into a shelter. The entire number of homeless dogs in the US is around thirty-five million.

"Bridget, you just totally amaze me, not just with the compassion you have, but also the knowledge you apparently have at your fingertips!

"Can we leave that in your very capable hands? Just let me know what kind of budget you will need. I give you the authorization of the CEO's office to set this in motion,"

This time the glowing smile was enough to warm the room.

Chapter Six

This is the last leg of my flight from LAX. We will be landing in about twenty minutes and I'm just hoping that someone remembers to come pick me up. Uncle Ray does drive. I have seen his car and believe me, that is not something one might forget. I mean, think about the mythical or historical God of the Sun, and warmth and all that, right. His car is a little bitty early two thousand Ford Fiesta which is bright yellow, just like the sun!

And upon my arrival at our regional airport, I saw the car as it circled the ramp just out front of the terminal. As I waited for my bag, Uncle Ray and Bridgette joined me. The later was near bursting with stuff she needed to share with me. And after surprising me with a bear hug, she let loose.

"Okay, per your instruction, we have had contracts written up with an offer to the city for the school building. But the really exciting thing is that we have found the farm building down on Commerce street.

"Why do you suppose that the street named Water Street is actually a block away from the water in the river and the street right on the river is Commerce Street? Seems it would be more accurate to have named them the reverse, but that's just me."

"I would guess that originally when the city was settled, Water Street was the one closest to the river but then at some later time, you know, like after the industrial revolution, factories were built along the river and they needed to add a street for those, and Commerce Street made perfect sense."

"Oh yeah. I guess that does make sense."

And that was the end of that history lesson. She was on to bigger and more pressing issues.

"Did you get the foundation set up?"

"No, not yet. I've been in California."

"Yeah, I know, but you spent half the time you were out there with lawyers, didn't you?"

"I want to create the corporate entity here in Virginia though. Cost too much on the west coast."

We had everything in tow and were by that point getting to the car.

"Uncle Ray, would you say your car is sunshine yellow?"

I couldn't resist the smirk with my gentle gouge. He didn't even notice.

"Actually, I'm more of the opinion it's canary yellow, but it is bright don't you think."

I think Bridgette got the meaning of my comment though. She changed the subject to avoid anyone feeling weird.

"I was going to pick you up, but my car is a pickup truck. We decided to come in Uncle Ray's, so we have more seats."

"No … wait. You have a pickup truck? And a driver's license?"

"Well, it would be against the law for me to drive without a driver's license you know."

I really need to get to know this young lady better. This means that she is at least sixteen years old if she has a license to drive in Virginia. Add that to the slowly growing list of things I have learned.

Of one thing we can all be certain, is that her energy level and the excitement she brings to any task. As soon as we were seated in the little car, she turned to look at me, filled with excitement.

"You'll have to tell us all about your trip to the west coast, but first I gotta tell you something that is amazing.

"You've been gone for five days, well almost, if you count today as a full day. While you were gone, Uncle Ray and I got us the farm building."

"You found a suitable building? Great. When can we look at it?"

"Any time we want, it's ours now. I mean, we own it!"

"What tha ..."

"No! Don't say that last word. It might bring bad luck."

"Well, please explain what you mean then."

"I found out about the building that is at the corner of Washington and Commerce Streets. It has been unused since 1953. A guy in Roanoke bought it about ten years ago for a song. When I investigated, I discovered that the city was about ready to seize the property for back taxes. The guy hasn't paid any for the last four years. He currently owes or rather owed ten thousand eight hundred fifty-seven dollars and twenty-nine cents including the interest and penalties. So, I contacted him and told him that we would take the responsibility of paying all the taxes, interest, and penalties to the city if he would just donate the property to our new foundation and we will even give him a receipt for a donation in the amount for which the building is currently assessed. And that is a hundred eighty-nine thousand eight hundred dollars. He can take that off his taxes which I guessed could save him as much as forty thousand dollars. Combined, that's over fifty grand and he paid less than that when he bought it, so he's ahead on everything. He had his lawyer draw up the papers that day and he overnighted them to me signed and witnessed by a notary.

"All we have to do is get a lawyer here to record them at the courthouse for us and the building is ours. Well, and of course, pay the city a few bucks. In fact, we were planning to go to the assessor's office and explain what was happening and ask them to hold off on the seizure for a month or so."

Okay, I'm a college professor as I've said, with two doctorates and I've not so far had a college student with this level of knowledge. My brain was screaming over this. I had to know.

"How can a sixteen-year-old know all of this stuff that you just spewed?"

My question did not even graze the surface let alone penetrate her inner defenses.

"Who said I'm sixteen years old?"

And that, as they say was the end of the conversation.

It didn't matter much that I'd gotten up and onto a flight that originated at 6:50 am Pacific time, spent five hours on one flight, transferred to another for nearly an hour and lost three hours arriving in Virginia at almost five in the afternoon, I needed to put together a plan for tomorrow before I settled down to unwind.

But the day did finally come to an end for me when they dropped me off at my house at five-thirty. We agreed to meet at the studio at nine the following morning. Beeep was extremely excited to get the paperwork filed so we would officially own the farm building. I grudgingly understood her position. Even though I was exhausted, I too, was excited that we had another step in the process taken care of and with shocking ease it seemed.

Once I dropped my bags in the bedroom, I went to my desk in the living room and made several notes on a legal pad for tomorrow.

1. Call Peter Davis, my lawyer, for an appt.
2. Call the city assessor's office.
3. Call the branch bank where I had transferred the estate funds.
4. Go to see the Farm building.
5. Look into hiring a handyman, building maintenance type of guy.
6. Get more info on Bridgette.

Yep, that should be enough to start at least the next week of activities. After a quick supper of tomato soup and a pimento cheese sandwich, I took a shower and crashed. Sleep took all of three minutes even though it was still before nine o'clock.

One nice thing about going to bed early was that I woke up before the obnoxious sound of the alarm blaring. And, I do have my priorities which sent me to the kitchen to put on a pot of coffee before getting dressed.

I rarely wear a necktie or even a suit for that matter since I teach young adults who more often than not, are wearing jeans and t-shirts or worse. But when I considered my potentials for the day, I did decide upon dress pants, a dress shirt, albeit with an open collar and a blazer to hopefully look like I knew what I was doing. I suspected … actually, hoped that I'd be seeing a lawyer, a banker, and a city official today.

My first stop was at the studio and as expected, Bridgette was waiting there for me. I was pleasantly surprised to see that she had made a pot of coffee with what was a brand-new drip machine.

"Hey Beeep, what's up?"

"Look at you! No jeans today. Must have important stuff to do."

"As a matter of fact."

I sat down at the desk I'd seemed to have assigned myself. I pulled out my pad and consulted the little list I'd done last night. Not only was it totally amazing that I'd thought to make a list and then actually done it, but I was even more shocked that I was able to successfully complete the first three items instantly without any difficulty.

I added to my notes the three appointments I'd set up. I was to see my banker first at 10:00 am and then Peter, my lawyer at 10:30. They were only a block apart. I saved the city assessor, a mister Dan Jenkins until after lunch at 1:30 pm. I was off to a good start for the day and to make things even nicer, Bridgette had fixed me a mug of coffee and when I looked up, she smiled at me as the set the cup on my desk and took a seat across from me.

"Thank you Bridge. Hey, we need to hire a good, reliable, talented, and hard-working Jack of all trades kind of a handyman. Know anyone like that?"

"No, but I do know a Colt of all trades. Will that work?"

The full force of the impish laughter made my morning. One of the things I like most about my current circumstances is the incredibly positive outlook of this young lady.

"Will he get upset if I call him Jack by mistake?"

Another burst of laughter.

"Prolly not! He has a journeyman's card in plumbing, electrical and he is a cabinet maker as a hobby. Plus, he is an accomplished welder with which he does art. He's good with his hands and smart too."

"If he's all that good why do you think he would be available?"

"He's still in school. Out at the community college."

"Oh, well, he may not want to go to work just yet."

"No, he has already asked if he can help us. He's sorta my ah … boyfriend."

"Does he have enough time?"

"Yeah, he only goes to school part-time, and he wants to keep going part-time until he gets two or three degrees. Right now, though, he's just taking welding classes and some math courses. He wants to be an engineer. Not the kind that drives a train although he probably would enjoy that too."

"How old is he?"

"Old enough to know better and young enough not to care, why?"

"I mean, is he old enough to do construction work on his own?"

"He's got a driver's license and those professional licenses, so I'd say yeah he is old enough. I'll call him and get him to come by and talk to us."

"Okay, but not today. Got enough on the schedule already. In fact, you said you have the papers for the farm building. I'm going to the lawyer in a few minutes, so give them to me if they're here."

Four minutes later I was in my car heading first to the bank and then Peter's office with the bill of sale and deed in hand. Bridgette didn't kid about this sort of stuff it seems.

My first stop was at the bank where I confirmed that the funds from California has been made available in the account I'd opened before my trip out west. Fortunately, I had some blank checks without any information printed on them other than the routing number and the account number for the checking account. I would be able to at least pay the taxes on the farm building. I did tell Wyatt, the banker that I would bring our logo art back in a few days to order checks. That done, I headed to my attorney's office.

I only needed enough time with the lawyer to turn over the creation papers for the not for profit to be incorporated in Virginia and the property paperwork to get the Commerce Street building recorded in the name of the foundation.

Peter had done the research based on a phone call I'd made to his office before leaving for Los Angeles and to my great relief, the foundation name was available in the Commonwealth until we filed to reserve it which he had also done for me.

Within fifteen minutes, I had signed the incorporation paperwork and it had been notarized by his paralegal. We would be the N-gener-8

Agronomics Foundation and would operate as a 501(C)(3) nonstock corporation. Peter explained to me that this designation meant that the foundation would have no owners but rather members and trustees as designated in the original paperwork and as maintained by a board of trustees which would have a chairman. Since there are no owners, the foundation does not technically own any assets.

As a result, the hard assets would have to be owned by another 501(c) (3) that was listed in the original filings as a member and fortunately he had also created that one as WCBII, LLC (for my initials Warwick Cottoway Blaire II) and that organization was the charge trustee for the foundation.

Even with the extra paperwork, I still managed to get out of his office before noon and headed back to the studio. I did stop on the way and pickup lunch for three people. And just coincidentally, there were three of us there to enjoy the Tea Room meal.

As we ate around the breakroom table, we talked about what had been done and what still needed to be done if possible, today. Uncle Ray liked the idea that the foundation would not own anything.

"It seems purer and more selfless that way."

"I'd like to go to see the farm building after I get back from the assessor's office. Also, Bridgette, will you use your laptop and develop a couple or three different business cards that we can vote on and then send out to be made. We're going to need that sooner than I thought we could get here."

"Sure, green on white stock? Also, I'll do a letterhead. Do we use this address or the farm building or do we get a post office box?"

"I hadn't thought about that. While we're at it, let's decide on a name for this space and a name for the farm and should be get a company or foundation phone number? Or two or three? And I suppose at least one of them should be toll free."

Suddenly, it was time to get to the assessor's office. I checked my inside jacket pocket and confirmed that I had a checkbook there and I headed outside to my car and my 1:30 appointment.

I realized as I entered city hall that I would probably be visiting here more often as a result of the foundation and its relationship with the city government. I stopped at a receptionist station in the central lobby and was directed to Dan Jenkin's office. It was not until I actually arrived at the mahogany door with the crazed glass and gold lettering that I realized that he is actually an elected official with the title of City Treasurer,

He turned out to be a pretty nice guy who was an alum of my university, and we were probably destined to have a good working relationship. He had his assistant print me a copy of the tax bill on the farm building and listened intently as I told him of our plans for its use.

He made one suggestion that I like instantly. I could request of city council a reduced tax rate since we were operating as a not for profit and to benefit the city.

I left the office nearly eleven thousand dollars less wealthy than when I had come in, but it seemed a small price to pay. I was on my way to see the actual farm but decided to make a stop by the main post office which was only a block away from city hall. Our first mailing address was going to be P.O. Box 1300. Not bad at all!

Chapter Seven

A new Monday morning and the first thought that jumped into my head was that I am a college professor and pretty soon the new semester would be beginning. How in the world could I continue to do all of this foundation stuff and teach three or four courses this coming semester? I couldn't. It was that simple. I had to get by the college and talk with the dean and make some sort of arrangements.

Fortunately, I am tenured and have not taken a sabbatical in several years. So it was that I explained to the dean what had happened with the death of my aunt and by only slightly bending the facts, I told him about the foundation that "my aunt's estate" had founded and that I was left as the only administrator. That wasn't bending the truth too much.

It was just believable enough to have the dean say that he would do everything in his power to get a last-minute sabbatical approved for me.

It was nearly noon when I arrived at the studio. Beep was there but Ray was not.

"Mornin' boss!"

That near giggle grin covered her face.

"Hey, if anything, you're my boss here. You have had the lead all along. Speaking of that, just how is it that you always know just what to do the keep moving forward?"

"Could be that I'm just smart, you know, a walkin' encyclopedia"

"Riiiight! So, what are we doing next?"

"Oh, well, I think we should go to see the farm. Colt said he would meet me there with pizza for lunch at about twelve-thirty. You wanna?"

We had come to the farm building in my very high-end Volvo XC90. Of course, on my professor's salary it should be way out of my league. What can I say though, I've always liked high end stuff. Back to reality though, it is ten years old and just turned two hundred thousand miles. Ergo, it was in my price range when I bought it last year.

When I pulled into what had once been a parking lot, just to the right side of the building, there was already another car there. A pretty sturdy looking young man climbed out as we arrived.

Beeep jumped out and gave him a hug and a peck on the check before turning that smiling face to me.

"This is Colt Drayford, my boyfriend. Colt I want you to meet Doctor Blair, my … well, I guess business partner or maybe benefactor?"

The young man turned to me and smiled broadly offering his right hand which I took to shake. He was for sure, sturdy and he shook with what almost seemed to be gratitude.

"Please to meet you Colt. I understand that pretty much if it needs fixing, you can fix it."

He started nodding at the fixing, and again flashed that smile.

"I might not be able to do it right away, but I'll fix it before I give up. Yes sir."

"I'll assume that Beeep here has told you what our plans are?"

"Yes sir. I think it's a great idea and a great thing to do."

"Would you be available to offer your services … at a competitive compensation of course."

"I'd love it. Right now, I'm working 12-hour days except for the ones when I have classes. So, a change in definitely in order."

"May I ask what you are currently earning per hour?"

He seemed almost embarrassed but with only a brief hesitation responded.

"Just above minimum wage. I'm earning eight bucks an hour."

I was truly astounded by that.

"I was thinking more like fifteen dollars per hour and a flexible schedule as long as you can get in forty hours per week."

"Last week I worked sixty-one hours and still managed to get in my school time, so yeah, I think I could do that."

"When would you be able to start?"

"How 'bout right now? I'll let my other two jobs know after I leave here today. It won't take more than a couple of days to be done with them both."

I offered my hand to shake on the deal, again being rewarded with that grin of pleasure on his face and I also noted that Beep was clapping her hands silently.

"Let's go inside this place so we can see what sort a bite we've taken on to chew."

The building is located on the eastern end of Commerce Street. To give you the perspective, the three streets from the river south are Commerce, then Water Street and then Main Street. Main is the longest of them starting at First Street and ending at 18th Street. Water starts at 4th and ends at 13th and Commerce starts at 6th and ends in the 1200 block. The numbers of the properties are all even on the north sides and odd on the south sides. They start with 100 and 101 and jumps up to the next hundred at the next cross street. Our studio is the first building in the 1300 block and is on the north side of main, so the address is 1300 Main Street.

On Water Street there is no 1300 block and the same is the case on Commerce. The address of the farm building we had just acquired was 1290 to indicate that it was the complete end of the addresses in that bock.

However, I'd been given a plat map of the property at the treasurer's office and even though 13th Street was never finished beyond Water Street, it was on the map. They are referred to as paper streets. Still, that gave me a great idea.

You see, the fact that I was able to get the post office box 1300 was because I asked if it was available, and it was. The postal worker told me that most people didn't want it because of the 13. My lucky day because our street address is also 1300. And now, coincidentally our farm building was at what should have been 1300 Commerce Street. An omen for sure.

"One of the first things I'd like you to do Colt, is make us a wrought iron sign to hang above the door here with some frills and the number 1300.

"We are going to change the address from 1290 to 1300 and then we'll notify the post office that it's been changed and then we'll tell the city of the new address.

"I figure if we don't ask, then there won't be any problem with doing it. Besides, who would really give a damn anyway?"

At some point I'll share with them that my dad's favorite lucky number was 13 and I had sort of adopted it as my own as well. Now both of our locations would be at 1300 and our PO Box was 1300. That is a bunch of good omens.

I was surprised that the building was in relatively solid condition considering how long it had been abandoned for all practical purposes. Sure, there was a lot to be done but the structure itself was rock solid from every indication.

"The first thing we're going to do it get a structural engineer in here and confirm that the place won't fall down on us. Then we will create plans for the conversions that will have to be done. We will also want completely new electrical, and all plumbing replaced.

"Colt, I'll leave getting quotes for those things to you, with you deciding on how much you want to do yourself and how much we need to contract for. The first thing on our plan might be that we determine a deadline for when we want the place to be ready to produce."

Beeep burped a giggle and added.

"Produce produce!"

"That is the plan, right?"

They both nodded affirmatively and started looking around on the first floor.

"Okay, let me share some details with you two.

"I have a set of plans and a plat for the property that I got at the treasurer's office when I paid the back taxes.

"We have just over half an acre, fifty-four one hundredths to be exact. It is one hundred sixty feet along the street and goes to the river's edge of approximately one hundred fifty-two feet depending on the height of the water at any given time. Incidentally, we're about twenty-one feet above water level here. Back in August of 1969 when hurricane Camille came through, Commerce Street was flooded in about three feet of water. So, it can happen.

"There is a basement which is the size of the main floor. In addition to this main floor there is a second floor that is exactly the same size and shape. Then for the floors three, four, five and six, the bump on the right front drops down too just thirty by fifty feet. Finally, the top two floors don't have the bump out on the eastern end.

"The building is one hundred forty feet along Commerce Street and on the west end is one hundred thirty-six feet deep. On the east end where the main entrance from the parking lot is located, the side wall goes back seventy feet and then there is a rear wall on the north side that is fifty feet before getting to the remainder of the eastern side which is then sixty-six feet to the rear of the structure.

"There is a total of just shy of one hundred eleven thousand square feet with the basement level and a full first and second floors. Then for floors three through six the east addition is smaller by two thousand square Feet. The top two floors, eight and nine do not have the east wing addition at all.

"The basement level which is accessible on the rear has a loading dock and I suspect we'll use that level for refrigeration and shipping and receiving. Main floor offices in the eastern addition and the remaining space will be set up like greenhouses with about four tiers of growing space.

"I did a few calculations and figured that we could have about seven and a half acres of truck garden and if I'm right in my guessing that we could do about four growing cycles each year, that should allow us to produce the equivalent of a thirty-acre farm."

Chapter Eight

Suddenly a week had blown by and once more it was Monday but, this week I had nothing on my mind but the foundation. We have a complete and comprehensive plan with schedules for the farm building and several contractors already working there. The roof is being done over and the interior of the building has been virtually gutted to the brick walls and the concrete floors, and the steel ceiling studs.

I thought I was getting into the studio early, at about seven twenty but to my surprise, not, Beeep and Colt were already there, and the coffee pot was hot but almost empty. I could hear them talking as I came up the stairs to our floor.

When I entered the office, Colt immediately stood and came toward me with his hand extended to shake. This was something he did every time he and I interacted. He was respectful to a fault, but I continue to hope he will become more relaxed around me as we work together.

"Morning sir. I have an idea I'd like to run past you."

"Sure."

I pulled out my desk chair and took a seat and he remained standing as if doing a presentation.

"I think I could do much more of the needed upgrades at the farm building with some help. Now, I don't want to get into budget problems though, so I had this idea.

"The community college has a number of trade programs and in many of them there is a huge advantage to have an internship of some sort. Suppose we created say a plumbing internship and an electrical internship and maybe some others as well. We would need to have insurance coverage like workers' compensation insurance.

"Most internship programs are not paid but offer credit hours at school. If we could do a couple or three-hour internship that allowed them to work on our projects for a semester for like ten or twelve hours per week. I can supervise them in three different categories. We do two good things at one time."

"That my friend, is a brilliant idea. And since I am a college professor, I can be the administrator and that should satisfy any academic requirements. Set aside a couple hours this afternoon and we will draft a proposal with a program description. When we are satisfied with it, we will take it out to the community college and meet with the president. When we have that support, we can go to the Office of the Chancellor of the Commonwealth Community College System to get that approval and endorsement.

I was amazed at the lack of red tape and the small number of roadblocks we encountered on the following Monday when I called the president of the local community college with our internship program offer.

The eagerness that met our idea was very satisfying as was the offer to meet with me at my earliest convenience in order to draft the program design. The president informed that he would then endorse the program and seek approval through the State Chancellor of the Community College System. He was very positive that he could acquire the needed authorization.

I will inform Colt that his position title will be Buildings and Grounds Manager.

Now from our plan, se need to add a person or team to work directly with the homeless folks we would bring in to staff the actual farming activities.

Instantly my memories of growing up with a nanny who managed our household, provided nursing support to my grandmother who lived with us until she needed to move to a supported living home and even than our nurse/nanny saw her multiple times weekly on bath days and just to visit and give emotional support until her last day on earth.

Josephine Christian or as I called her, Pheney. She was and is my African American Momma. With a heart of gold and a passion to help those less fortunate, she still volunteers at a soup kitchen and used clothing store, Pheney exemplifies true Christian values even now while living on a small pension.

A twenty-minute telephone call to tell her what we are doing had her promise of full support. She and I were mutually happy to be working together again. I told her where our offices are located, and she said she would be there the following morning. With that we added our Residential Services Manager.

Per usual, I had been totally unaware of my stealthy little partner who had been listening keenly to my phone conversation, but when I finished with a smile on my face, she shared one of her delightful giggles with me, as well as another idea.

"You know, we have a pretty good skeleton put together here, but aren't we gonna need someone who knows about farming? I mean, we are going to build an indoor farm for our homeless workers to work in and grow organic crops to help feed themselves and to earn money to pay for all of this, right?"

"Why am I sure that is just the introduction for the answer that *YOU* already know?"

That bubble of laughter and her simply beautiful face makes me willing to do anything for her.

"I suspect that's because you know how smart I am!"

More giggles!

"And yes, I do have the answer already. My brother Jacob has a BS degree in agriculture with a focus in Environmental Horticulture with major studies in sustainable Vegetable Horticulture. He is now working on an MSLS. That's a Master of Science in Life Sciences including floriculture, urban horticulture, nursery production, pomology, and vegetable production. And that includes stuff like plant breeding and genetics, innovative approaches to intensify production and farm ecology. That is exactly what we are going to be doing. In fact, I got the idea from him."

"Well, the only remaining question is, will he join us?"

"I think that can be arranged. Sustainable agriculture is what he has dedicated his life too so far. And he is passionate about helping rid the earth of the homeless situation.

'Oh, and his hobby is baking. His bread is incredible!'

"Great! Then if you will, ask him to join us. And what is pomology?'

Another giggle.

"Oh that? It's the science of growing fruit. You didn't think it was reading *POLMS* did you?"

This time she bent over holding her stomach as she laughed her full-blown giggles.

I had known Jacob for as long as I had known Beeep. It came as no surprise that he had done so well in the academic world. The simple reason started with good genes and developed while living in a smart household and a supportive environment.

Suffice it to say that Jake jumped at the chance to work with us. And along with our newly approved trades internship which was the source of quite a bit of support and even excitement at the local community college as well as with the state-wide system. In a matter of weeks, our program had the first 8 interns ready to begin the program. Now we even had a board and an executive staff in all critical areas.

Our first organizational meeting held in early August saw us lay out a plan with each vital step outlined and an approach mapped.

The first steps were to renovate the now three buildings we had acquired. The former elementary school building would be converted to residential pods all of which would be serviced by the cafeteria for three meals each day and the auditorium to be used for training.

Next, the former factory building along the river would be converted for agricultural use, employing water from the river and solar collected by the converted roof of the building.

As we were wrapping up our first organizational meeting, the office phone rang. That in itself surprised me since only a very few people even knew we existed, let alone what our telephone number might be. Since I was seated nearest the phone, I picked up the receiver.

"Ingenerate Foundation. How may I help you?"

Fortunately, we had only moments ago approved the organizational name N-gener-8 Agronomy Foundation, so I at least had something with which to answer the call.

At the other end of the phone, a very pleasant female voice responded.

"Yes, is this the correct number for Wick Blaire?"

"Yes. This is Wick Blaire speaking."

"Great! Wick, this is Mary Martha Woodforde. I don't know if you remember me or not, but we were in the same graduating class in high school."

"Of course, I do! We were in several classes together. In fact, I think I irritated you because I most always called you May May!"

"That's me! And it did irritate me a little, but I grew to like it."

"Wow. The last I heard about you was that you had married a man from West Point and were living in like Montana. What can I do for you?"

"I think it is rather something I can do for you.

"I did marry a career Army officer. We live in Tacoma, Washington. I'm back in the hometown to settle my Dad's estate.

"He passed just over four months ago and since I am the sole heir, all of it was left to me."

"My condolences."

"Thank you. It turns out that when I met with our attorney here, Peter Davis who also went to high school with us, he told me about what your foundation is doing. Well, I am an advocate for the homeless in the Tacoma Seattle area. So, I have come up with a proposition for you.

"What would you say to my joining your efforts here and we expand it to a country-wide operation?"

"At the risk of sounding like Dumbo, I am all ears!"

We both laughed at that image for a brief moment.

"Great. Could we get together?"

"Absolutely. I'd really like that. How long are you going to be in town?"

"My schedule is very flexible. Still, I would like to get this started as soon as is humanly possible."

"I see. Well, I am in the office now, if you're available."

"Yes, I'd love to meet right now. I'm at Peter's office and he says you are in the old Seven Hills buggy factory building at 13th and Main?"

"We are. There is a door in the middle of the block on 13th between Main and Commerce. It's unlocked. Come on in and up to the second floor. That's where I am."

"Okay, see you in ten minutes."

I met Mary Martha as soon as she came in the door at the top of the stairs. I didn't hesitate but welcomed her with a hug.

"You haven't changed a bit!"

"Neither have you, other than that slight greying in your sideburns."

I slipped my hand onto her left elbow to guide her through the confusion that is our office until I could offer her a seat at our conference table with a gesture of my hand. I took the one on her left.

"I must say you sure did get my attention with 'that country-wide' comment. That is the ultimate goal of our operation. We would love to have a farm in most every major city. Tell me your idea."

"Please understand that I do not mean to be immodest when sharing this with you. As you may know my Dad and his family were into the tobacco industry when most people used tobacco products.

"First, Grandfather started the South City Tobacco warehouse down on Commerce Street. That burned down in the late 1930's. The Woodforde Tobacco Company then built a new three-level warehouse on Main and bought a building in Roanoke County where they introduced Woodforde Cigarettes.

"The warehouse on Main was a public tobacco warehouse where farmers brought their harvests to sell. The warehouse received a commission on all sales and purchased the leftover leaves for use by the company.

"Up on the upper level there was a drying room. The warehouse was on the main level and the lower level was a processing plant for chewing tobacco, snuff and pipe tobacco which was also sold for "roll your own".

"In 1951 Dad Built another warehouse in Nelson County. By 1960, the company was bringing in several million dollars each year and the book value of the company had increased about twenty-five times the original invested in 1930.

"All of that came to me with the estate. I don't have any need for any of the buildings nor do I want to invest the time dealing with selling them.

"So, when I was telling Peter, he suggested that you might be interested in them for your organization. Then he described what your group is all about.

"I decided right away that not only would I donate the real estate for the nice tax deduction but that I might try to con you into a seat on the board so that we could do the same thing out west."

"Not to question your ability or freedom to make the decision, but to avoid any potential problems, is you husband in agreement with this. The last thing I would want to do is stir up any animosity."

"I appreciate that, but being a forward thinker, I went there ahead of you. He not only is totally onboard but agrees to volunteer with the program when you come out west.

"He has one focused desire himself. He wants to see a nation where no veteran is ever homeless or hungry."

"That is super. Then, yes, I agree to your terms. Your husband, I don't even know his name."

"He is Mike Porter, Doctor Mike Porter. He is a general practitioner and semi-retired Hospital Administrator. He has an incredible story himself.

"He is an Army veteran and his goal in life is to feed, clothe, and offer residence until homeless veteran is no longer a thing that exists in the United States."

"I like this man already and I haven't met him yet. And do you think he would be willing to also take a seat on our board?"

"I'm confident he will accept immediately."

"Will you, as our director of fundraising be so kind as to make him the offer?"

May May nodded affirmatively as she picked up her cell phone. Having been raised by parents who taught me to be polite, I headed to our little kitchen to allow her some privacy. In no more than three minutes, she joined me. When I saw her wide smile, I assumed she had gotten a positive response.

"I have been here just long enough to have totally forgotten about the time difference. I interrupted his morning shower! Still, he accepted instantly.

"I told him my title and he asked to be our medical officer. I assured him that could be the case."

"Of course! Very good decision.

"Do you have time to tell me about Mike? Then perhaps, we could have lunch?"

"I've got about an hour before I need to leave for the airport. I can tell you about Mike but won't have time for lunch … at least, not this time."

The last comment was delivered with a dip of her head and a coy smile before offering a solid brief of her husband's profile.

"His name is Michael Kirk Porter III but he only answers to Mike. He is a retired US Army Colonel. His grandfather, Michael the first or as Mike calls him Michael the original, founded Porter-Grandville Fine chemicals which became Porter Pharmaceuticals. Then the Porter family enterprises expanded into developing hospitals and the like which became Porter Health Care Inc. Mike was being groomed to take over the family business, but he wanted nothing to do with corporate America. Mike chose a different route altogether. He graduated West Point and afterward attended Albany Medical College where his father and grandfather attended and were contributors.

"He was commissioned a second Lt. And since he was technically in the Army for the 9 years he was in school, he was able to retire eleven years later with the rank of Colonel In the Medical Corp. His last Army assignment was as Hospital Admin in Tacoma. Now he is semi-retired with a small private practice and is a volunteer at the VA hospital.

"As I said before, he is passionate about no veterans being homeless. He is a truly good man.

"We have a son and a daughter. That's us in a nutshell."

"He does sound like a good man and a great addition to our operation."

"The kids are the reason I want to get back home today."

"Have you been using a rental car or a ride sharing service while you've been here?"

"One of those ride things that Mike calls Goober!"

"Well, at least let me give you a ride to the airport."

"Now that is something I do have the time for!"

That was followed by a great chuckle.

Chapter Nine

As we neared the entrance to Preston Glenn Airport, I realized that the driveway to the terminal is divided, and the left or right option were dependent on which airline one is using.

"Which airline?"

"Oh, just stay on the main drive on to the far end of the terminal. I 'm flying Porter airlines."

"Wha …?"

"I'm flying my own plane."

"Like a corporate plane?'

"I guess, Mike and I have three airplanes and both of us fly."

"You're a pilot!"

"Yes, I am. When Mike and I got married, he had his license, and he insisted that for safety reasons I should at least know how to land the plane if something ever happened while we were up. So, I did the whole thing and now have a license and am instrument rated for multiple engines and we are both doing our final certification training for jet.

"Mike is addicted to flying and I caught the bug too. I've had a license now for what will be ten years in July.

"Now he wants a Gulfstream or a Cessna Citation. I like the Gulfstream better."

"Wow! And you can fly one of those?"

"Yep."

"What kind of plane do you have now?"

"We have three. A Cessna Skyhawk That I learned on, a Piper Seneca twin engine and the Piper Cheyenne I've got here with me."

"Have a good flight home and we'll be in touch."

When I arrived back at our studio there was paperwork transferring the former tobacco warehouses on Main Street and in Nelson County and two former cigarette factories.

"Beeep, where is Colt this morning?"

"He's down at the farm building meeting with three contractors. I can get him back up here after he is done down there if you want."

'Yeah, do that please."

Bridgette returned her attention to the phone conversation. It was obvious from the near whispered portions of what she was saying that the two are romantically involved. Finally, she ended the call with a little giggle and turned a radiant smile toward me.

"I assume you want to talk with him about the new buildings?"

"Yes. So, you saw the paperwork from the lawyer?"

"You have paperwork already?"

The look on her face was that of slight surprise.

"Yes. It's all right here."

"She really did it then? That's great. Now we can use the punch line 'coast to coast' for fundraising."

"Not so fast there! We aren't even operational here on the east coast yet."

"But we have a business plan and a board of directors who are capable and the seed money to be up and running in, oh, I'd say no more than sixty days.

"Then we can start with a facility in Tacoma or Seattle."

"Wait, how do you even know that we potentially have a connection in that area?"

She smiled at me with her left eyebrow tilted upward.

"I just know stuff sometimes. Like when I told you about your aunt in California."

"Care to share what you know about the Seattle Tacoma area?"

"I know that your old high school friend who just donated those buildings ..."

Beeep nodded toward the file folder on my desk that held the transfer deeds that had come down from Peter Davis' office this morning.

" ... lives in Tacoma. Right?"

"As a matter of fact, she does. But that doesn't mean anything in and of itself."

"And, I have the distinct impression that she as well as her husband are joining our board."

"As a matter of fact, that is true, but that doesn't guarantee our possibilities of expanding to the west coast."

"Let me share some more stuff that I just happen to know.

"Her husband is a doctor and heir to his family's trust. The husband's grandfather founded Porter-Grandville Fine chemicals 1883 which became Porter Pharmaceuticals in 1928. The Porter family enterprises began buying and developing hospitals and health centers/services over the next 25 years. The Porter Health Care Inc. was converted at the retirement of the husband's father in the 1955-1960 period to the Porter Health Trust, valued at hundreds of millions

USD. Her hubby is the 3rd generation to have attended Albany Medical College where his father and grandfather attended and were major contributors. Hubby's last assignment in the family Trust was as regional Hospital Admin in Tacoma. He is now semi-retired but still maintains a small private practice and is a volunteer at the VA hospital. His net worth is approximately five-hundred sixty-five million USD.

"He is totally absorbed with the desire to see that no US veterans are homeless, hungry or in need of healthcare."

"How do you know all this?"

She shrugged and that impish smile flashed briefly.

"I just do, you know."

Colt Drayford came strolling into the office just before three in the afternoon. On the fairly numerous occasions I have had the opportunity to spend time with this burly young man, I have found him to be polite, kind, and hard working.

I knew for example that he had worked twenty to thirty hours a week since high school to assist his mother with expenses and most recently to pay for his education without creating any debt. When Bridgette had suggested that he would be the right person to coordinate the work that our buildings would need, I was more than pleased to have him help us, particularly since that would help him to continue his education toward a BS in engineering in the process.

His report that day re-confirmed that my decision to add him to our organization was the correct call.

We now had a plan that described the kind of projects for each of our original locations and the order in which they should be done, as well as projected overall budgets for each of those renovations. He had also created a sensible schedule as to which buildings would be ordered so that our staffing additions might be done in a practical order.

The residential building would logically be first, followed by the staffing needed for that facility, then the original agro-facility so the needed staffing there could be determined and filled. Finally, a more long-term plan for the newest buildings and the possibilities that will surely lie ahead for the foundation.

What really amazed me was that Colt included as part of his project plan, using a portion of what had been employee parking and surface treated basketball and tennis courts around the school building to be converted to a drive-through carwash.

He proposed that we contract with the local government and multiple corporate entities to provide cleaning services for automotive equipment, again using residents to staff those services as well.

"Colt, I am both impressed and pleased with you thoughts and ideas."

"Thanks Doc. Bridgette told me you are open to ideas. Everywhere I've ever worked has always seemed to look down on my ideas since I'm young."

"One of the best things I've learned from teaching is that almost every original idea is worthy of consideration. When you analyze it, every positive result starts with an idea."

"Sure! That's cool. Thanks. Oh, and Bridgette said she would be here at eleven-thirty. She has some information for you."

With that the young man nodded and left my office. I realized that I was hungry, and thoughts of a bacon cheeseburger invaded my mind. I checked my watch to find that Beeep would be here in less than ten minutes, so lunch would have to wait.

Almost immediately, I heard the sweet sounds of her voice and seconds later after a single knock on my door her smiling face appeared through the slight opening.

"Hi. Figured you might be hungry, so I brought you a burger and fries."

She handed me a burger-doodle bag. Even though I should be long passed it by now, I was still shocked when I opened it to find a bacon cheeseburger and an order of fries.

"How do you do this ... never mind.

"Colt said you have some new information for me?"

She sort of shrugged and took a seat in the side chair across from me.

"Yeah. Those two newest board members, your old high school friend who gave us those tobacco warehouses. You know, the one who is married to the heir to Porter Pharmaceuticals and Health Care are about to do something else that's really nice and is going to be very helpful.

"You see, the good doctor is a really loyal veteran himself and he has always felt guilty about his family's wealth, particularly when there are between seventy and eighty thousand homeless vets in the United States at present.

"He is consumed with a drive to end homelessness for U. S. military veterans.

"It is interesting to note that Los Angeles city and LA County, CA, at a total count of over sixty-three thousand homeless, ranks that area at second in the US, and first for homeless veterans with approximately five thousand of those homeless in the area being veterans.

"In his efforts to provide assistance for those veterans, over the last two years, the Porter Trust has acquired Ginger Florence High School in the Huntington area, in Los Angeles County. Ginger Florence HS is a four-story masonry facility of twenty-four thousand square feet with athletic fields, parking lots and two twelve hundred square foot greenhouses on just under fifteen acres and a second facility, Grayson Royal High School, a twenty-one thousand square foot brick and mortar three-story building on just under four acres for the combined cost of six hundred thirty-three thousand five hundred dollars.

"This was done with the intention of providing shelter, food and healthcare for veterans.

"And now that Doctor Porter has joined our organization, it seems appropriate that those facilities will come under our organizational plan."

"How do you know about all of this Bridgette?"

"I'm the one who got him started."

Another of those Beeep mysteries to add to my growing list.

Chapter Ten

It was a Friday morning in August when the complete board of directors for our organization met to review status of our facilities and to develop the implementation of the actual working activities.

Over the several months we had been developing the overall organization, our initial founding members had evaluated the positions we needed to fill, for the foundation to grow and flourish.

Even though we may still need additional staff and leadership in the not-too-distant future, at the time of that meeting, there was a level of confidence with our current advisors and staff.

In the past two months, we were pleased to add very capable individuals to our organization and our board of directors.

Although I shouldn't have been, I *was* surprised when I got to the office to find that Colt had been there helping set up for our meeting. The three conference tables from the offices had been moved out into the common space and arranged end to end with about fourteen chairs spaced around them. My own desk chair was at the end closest to the two offices and obviously meant for the chairman, or me as is the case.

Coffee as well as tea iced and hot was awaiting the desires of our members. Within less than thirty minutes of my arrival, individuals began joining us. There were several faces with whom I was familiar and several new ones. I would find out, however, that they were not strangers.

Among the familiar faces were Uncle Ray and Phiney Cunningham, the supervisor of residential care at our converted elementary school, and Beeep's brother Jacob who is our agricultural leader.

I was quickly able to put together the newer faces with folks whom I'd talked with through email, Zoom meetings and official contracts making four of them new board members for our organization.

First among them was Dr. Mallory Barrett the new Executive Vice President of Horticulture and agronomics who was absorbed in conversation with Pat Lindstrom our Culinary Natural and Organic Foods Chef. The two foodies had only met each other during those video calls and would be a self-contained team.

Last to arrive was our new Vice President and director of communications, Chelsea Grant.

"Good morning, and welcome to the founding meeting for the Board of Directors for our effort which we have named The Ingenerate Agronomics Foundation. This was selected because the word "ingenerate" means to engender or give rise to, create naturally, organically if you will. Since we are going to cause to exist, to develop by not only growing products, but creating assistance to those in need by providing a home to a certain number of homeless, and to create jobs for them and therefore create a better future for them. The agronomics portion is to create plants for food and restoration. Our intention The founding trio of Bridgette, Uncle Ray and I created an organization that is focused on both helping homeless people to reinvent their lives through first having a roof over their heads and helping to provide for themselves and others in the same or similar situations through building self-esteem and retraining them for a productive role in society. A major ingredient in this process will also be hydroponic farming to raise organic vegetables and developing a market that will be self-supportive. While in the program, each person will be trained in a job related to either assisting in the housing facilities or the agricultural activities.

Perhaps, it would be helpful if I introduced everyone here today so we can avoid the whole strangers wasting time and curiosity.

"I am Doctor Warwick Blair. I am your CEO and Chairman of the Board. Now, I'll start here on my immediate left and go around the table. I'm going to brag about each one of you as well.

"First is our buildings and grounds Manager, Colt Drayford. Colt is licensed as a journeyman plumber and electrician and a certified welder. He is also currently a college student working toward a BA degree in architectural engineering.

"To Colt's immediate left Josephine Cunningham. Phiney is and always has been powerful mentally and is a momma bear when it comes to her family and extended family once they get to know her and love her. That extended family included mine as I was growing up. She will be our residential Manager.

"Next is Chelsea Grant our Director of Communications. With a BA in Media and Culture Randolph Macon Woman's College and an MPhil/PhD in Media and Communications from The London School of Economics and Political Science, Chelsea will also sit on our Board.

"To Chelsea's left is Mallory Barrett who prefers Mal. With BS, MS, PhD degrees in Horticulture, botany and plant biology. She is to serve on the board and as Executive VP of Horticulture and Agronomics.

"As you may or may not know, horticulturists are actively involved with botany and plant biology: Mal's Bachelor of Science is in Agricultural Business which combined core undergraduate courses in agricultural economics with basic business management and agricultural science foundation courses as well as Plant Science/Crop Production. That was followed an MS in Agricultural Science at Cal State University Fresno and finally a PhD from the University of California Berkeley in Agricultural and Resource Economics and the professional title of Agronomist.

"Next as we come up this side of the table is Patrick Lindstrom. Pat is an Organic Foods Chef who has earned a Bachelor of Professional Studies in Culinary Science at Culinary Institute of America. He also holds a Master of Science in Food Science and Technology from Ohio State with a comprehensive curriculum covering areas such as sensory science, advanced food processing, food chemistry, food packaging, and functional foods for health.

And last, but not least, Yale G. Waterman who is a Retired educational software/systems developer. Yale was the founder of Waterman

Technology. He has a BA in education, an M Ed and MS and D.Ed. in Upper education. After teaching for 12 years, he left the classroom but remained a public education advocate and an educational software/systems developer for eighteen years before retiring. He was sole owner of Waterman Technology which he sold at his retirement.

"Here on my right are my two co-founders of Ingener8, Bridgette and Uncle Ray.

"Finally, we have two Board members who are not present here today. And they are Doctor Michael Porter III and his wife, Mary Martha Porter, A lady who was a member of my high school graduating class as Mary Martha Woodforde. She recently returned to our hometown to settle her father's estate. Her father was Walter Roland Woodforde, the past President and CEO of Olde Virginia Tobacco here in the city. Mary Martha is his sole heir and has donated to our organization multiple tobacco warehouse buildings that are no longer in use. Doctor and Mrs. Porter live in the Tacoma/Seattle area and when they heard about our plans, decided that they would like to create another agronomic homeless program in Washington, based on our model.

"Now, I will relinquish the floor to Colt Drayford for a report on our physical farm and residential buildings."

He nodded to me and stood.

"Thank you Doctor Blair. As mentioned a few minutes ago, I am the Manager of Buildings and Grounds. We are in the process of converting the old Garland Armstrong Elementary School. The building is being refitted as a residential dorm, that will use the existing rest rooms on each floor, to which we will be adding showers, as well as the cafeteria for meals. The auditorium will be a massive training room to reintroduce the skills of job search, and others that will be determined as needed through Interviewing our residents as they move into the facility. Regular training will also take place to prepare our residents to work in our vertical farm building.

"That vertical Farm building is also currently being converted in stages that will include the installation of rooftop solar panels and batteries with which the building will be powered. Since the building is located at 1290 ... or rather 1300 Commerce Street along the river, we can and will use river water for irrigation.

Frontage of the site is one-hundred seventy-three feet by one hundred forty-five feet deep and lot is point five seven three acres or twenty-five thousand eighty-five square feet. Inside, the building will provide one-hundred twenty-two thousand four-hundred square feet or the equivalent of two point eight one acres of "farming Space" on the dix upper floors. The basement will be set up for utility rooms and temporary storage as well as shipping. There is already a shipping dock on the river side of the building.

The facility, in its present state, has the building which was condemned and valued at forty-six thousand three-hundred dollars and land at one-hundred forty-three thousand five-hundred dollars based on real estate tax assessment. We were able to acquire the property from the last owner for agreeing to pay the five years of unpaid taxes and related penalties. The total amount paid for this property was ten-thousand eight-hundred fifty-seven dollars and twenty-nine cents which was a great deal based on the tax assessment at the time of purchase. After renovation is completed, we are projecting the market value to increase to approximately three point two million dollars.

"This renovation is expected to be done in approximately two months or perhaps less.

"We were also just notified that those buildings donated by the Woodforde Trust are three tobacco warehouses. One of those is here in town while two others are elsewhere in the state. We plan to travel to those facilities on Monday to evaluate the best use of those buildings and then to add them to our plans.

"As I mentioned, the commerce Street location will offer us almost three acres of growing space."

Suddenly Bridgette was standing just to the right of Colt and in her typical near excited voice added an idea that was totally new.

"Hello folks, I'm Bridgette and I just want to add one small feature. And that is a number of trained service dogs who will help with anxiety, PTSD, and other similar potential difficulties our residents might experience will be at our residential facilities. This was approved by our CEO."

And with that she nodded to the board members and was gone in an instant.

The next member to speak was Mal Barrett, our VP of Agronomics.

"Will the building be ready to begin our first planting cycle then?'

"In the two months, do you mean? Yes ma'am. The tiers will be built as will the plumbing for irrigation and all the solar lamps will be installed and tested. The heating system for the total building will be operational by Monday. Thermostats will be set at 62 degrees on the growing floors as advised by Mister Lindstrom.

"In fact, Doctor Barrett, if you would be willing to meet with me at the farm building on Monday, we can talk with the construction crew about the design of the planting tiers to provide for maximum exposure to the created sunlight."

"Yes, I would like to do that. And while I'm there, might you give me a tour?"

"I'd be glad to! Can you meet me at say, ten am?"

"I'll see you then."

I was also curious about something.

"Mal, if Colt can work with you and perhaps with a design in mind, might you be able to predict yields for that location?"

"I can already give you a pretty good estimate, Wick."

"Once again I find myself at the risk of being imagined Dumbo, still, I'm all ears!"

"We have discussed the vegetables easiest to grow in multiple "seasons" or cycles for the best end crop yields. They are radishes, carrots, asparagus, broccoli, onions, celery, squash, spinach, tomatoes, bell peppers, Irish potatoes, and sweet potatoes.

"After visiting the farm building, seeing the layout and getting measurements, I'll be able to calculate yields. Then I can calculate anticipated income based on current market prices.

"Do we have a dedicated finance person yet?

"No, we don't at present, but my old grad school roommate is on my short list for CFO. I'll get that taken care of in the next day or three."

Chapter Eleven

Just as it does every week, Monday started off at a busy pace. I knew that Colt was at the farm building on Commerce, monitoring and advising the four contractors who would be there for this and several weeks to come.

Also, this morning our VP of Agronomics would have her first tour and begin to work with Pat Lindstrom, our Chief Organic Chef to develop growing plans for the facility.

It was expressed at the Board meeting that we needed a projection for actual crop production along with related costs as well as potential income so that an operational budget could be created.

I have asked Mal and Pat our foodies to stop by the office this afternoon after their tour to chat with John Viken and me, John was my graduate school roommate and has over the years become my brother from a different mother. He is of Norwegian heritage and his surname has its origins from the Scandinavian word meaning "strength" and that totally suits who he is. JBV as I have known him for all these years, has agreed to serve as our Chief Financial Officer. His plan was to come by to pick up some raw data to begin creating budgets and an operational plan with me.

Of course, I'm waiting for feedback from our agro group after they have seen the actual "farm" space.

It was almost six pm when we finished what I had expected would be a fairly quick and simple get together. We had used the conference table in my office. That turned out to be the perfect venue for our meeting. There was one thing for sure that would come as a result though. JBV would need an office really soon and it would need desk, a conference table, and a few dozen filing cabinets.

Colt told me he has seen just the right stuff at a used furniture shop in the next block and that he would make the buy in the next day or two. First, he said he would start tomorrow and frame the actual office space next to mine and get the drywall guys from the farm building to finish the walls and trim. Colt said that even if he had to come in over the weekend, he'd get it painted and the same interlocking vinyl floor that looks just like a grey oak hardwood laminate that is in the two offices that are already in our "studio/clubhouse". He assured me that in a week, he would have the office and furniture in place.

And one week later it was a reality. The used furniture was a desk, two dark wooden bookcases with glass doors and three four drawer matching file cabinets.

When JBV returned, he had a nice place to work. He had also prepared projections for income and expenses for the next one-hundred eighty days.

As he explained it to me, our agro group has projected yields of six tons of radishes, just under ten tons of carrots, two tons of asparagus, over three and a half tons of broccoli, ten tons of onions, sixteen tons of celery, six and a half tons of assorted squashes along with five and a half tons of tomatoes included with several other organic vegetables representing an annual revenue of two hundred eighteen thousand dollars.

"Each of the six floors will specialize in two plants with multiple growing cycles each calendar year. We are still determining our costs for that same timeframe. At this point, we have calculated that amount to be approximately sixty-five thousand, leaving a gross margin of just over one hundred fifty thousand for the first full year of operations.

"And it is our plan, to be adding at least three new operations over the following year. The Foundation already has physical plants that will accommodate that first round of expansion.

"We have gotten our legal incorporation licenses and Internal Revenue Service approval and authorization as a 501 (C-3), making our earnings tax exempt.

"This classifies us as a charitable organization, allowing us to solicit donations as well as corporate sponsorships, making those tax deductible as well.

"When these projections are fully evaluated and tested, we will offer a written report with projections for multiple years.

"At the moment, based on the numbers I have seen, I'd say you're pretty much open to do most anything you want."

Chapter Twelve

That organizational Board meeting was little more than a memory. In reality, the forty-two months that have passed have resulted in vast and significant changes in our operations. The major change is that we are now legitimately a national organization with multiple facilities in Virginia, the District of Columbia, South Carolina, and most recently on the west coast in three states and best yet, we are still expanding. Our newest operations are in the Los Angeles and Seattle areas.

One of our better meetings had resulted in an organizational plan that became a reality within that calendar that it all started. Four months after that first get together, the structure determined how often the Board of Directors would meet on a normal basis, allowing for special needs for any additional unplanned meetings to address exceptions that would surely arise. An executive management structure was created and empowered to make routine and special circumstances decisions along with day-to-day operations.

The question was raised, "What will the organization need? The first and most obvious answer that any community college business student would offer to that query is that some sort of management structure needed to be created.

In a positive move, an executive management group made up of a Chief Financial Officer, a Chief Operations Officer, Chief Executive Officer, a Corporate Legal Officer/Counsel was addressed by creating job descriptions and appropriate titles and empowering those positions, with the approval of executive staff to create the needed support staff in each department.

When this dust settled, we discovered that we had already covered all those executive positions with only one vacancy remaining. We needed an on staff legal team. The senior legal officer position was recruited and filled. Kimberly Andrews, a Juris Doctorate graduate of UCLA law and an LLM graduate of the London School of Economics had heard of us and volunteered to start as a pro-bono attorney and to give us ten hours each week until the organization grows to the point we can afford to hire her full-time. Kim is the granddaughter of two attorneys, one of whom was a member of SCOTUS as well as a third-generation partner of McVicker's, Arthur and Andrews, a law firm founded in 1864. Her mother was a district Court Judge and partner in the firm founded by that grandfather. Since Kim is a fourth generation in the family law practice she is afforded the freedom to pursue worthy causes such as our organization with the hearty approval of her primary employer, a very civic minded group itself.

It was then suggested and approved that the executive management team would hold a status meeting every Monday morning to review the results of previous goals and, based on where the organization landed on the results curve, to then establish objectives for the immediate and coming future goals, to review needs and allocate the necessary funding and coordination to pursue those next priorities.

The newly minted legal department not only proved to be worthwhile in drafting contracts and the typical stuff done by legal departments, but through the natural curiosity of an inquisitive brain like the one that got our VP of legal through multiple law degrees, she began a research drive through any potential sources that could contribute to our growth.

The first result her inquisitive mind achieved is that the federal Government Services Administration was the potential source of physical facilities that might be available at reasonable acquisition costs.

She discovered that former federal facilities that were no longer being used were turned over to the GSA for sale. These buildings might have been post offices, federal court houses, federal office buildings like FBI offices or labs and even military facilities. It is shocking to learn that the federal government occupies more than four-hundred eighty thousand physical locations in the United States that range from parking lots to military bases.

At any given point in time upward of seventy-five thousand of these locations are at the very least grossly under used, with many deteriorated to the point of being unusable without renovation.

The GSA has great difficulty in the disposal of these under used and in many instances completely unused facilities. The lack of cooperation in Congress leads to a gross lack of funding to do the badly needed renovations thus leaving these facilities unusable for their intended purposes. At any given time, hundreds of locations are not in use and as a result are relegated to surplus status.

Disposing of the properties is greatly burdened by a wealth of bureaucratic red tape. The ultimate outcome is that on any day, hundreds of facilities might be empty and classified as surplus and they may remain in that status for multiple years. And to make things even more difficult, there are policies that detail the extensive regulatory requirements that must be met before the sale of these properties. There must be a certain minimum level of repairs including any needed environmental remediation to reach compliance for sale. One positive for our organization is that we are now an approved non-profit involved in assisting the homeless.

That allows us to be on an approved vendor list whenever these asset sales are made. Being a member of that list over the past four years has afforded the organization the chance to bid on more than a dozen sales of former federal properties.

It was certainly near shocking to discover the numbers of physical plant facilities owned by the federal government. That surprise was totally minimized by the discovery that surplus included more than six hundred twenty million acres of land! No, that wasn't a mistake, nearly three-quarters of a billion acres of land! The land in question is used or at least held by the federal government as runoff for major dam projects, lands reserved for environmental barriers, parks and more. As use of these sites decline, the option is always available for sale of certain acreages.

Over the nearly five years since our first organizational board meeting, our foundation has acquired just over fourteen-thousand acres of land. It is our plan, which is in progress, to add both beef and chicken open range facilities on those properties.

The recommended standards for free range chicken ranching are to allow two and a half acres per thousand birds with space for hen houses every four-hundred yards. An open range chicken ranch for five thousand chickens, which is five-hundred forty-four thousand five-hundred square feet or a plot of approximately 245 by 240 yards with a hen house in the center.

This facility could produce seven-hundred fifty thousand organic/free range eggs each year. Additionally, over each six months, half of the laying hens are replaced and harvested for meat, thereby generating seven-thousand pounds per year for each chicken ranch plus sixty-two thousand five hundred dozen eggs.

Our organization now has twelve such chicken ranches in six different states, with each of these states having either two of these ranches, or a "double size" chicken ranch. Each of the ranches provides a place of residence, and employment for 12 to 15 formerly homeless, covering all costs of operations and generating funds to be used elsewhere.

Chapter Thirteen

In addition to the chicken ranches, another branch of our operations is represented by the two-thousand-acre beef ranches held in each of nine central and western states. In a typical year, on these eighteen thousand acres of pastureland we manage a typical total of seventy-four thousand eight hundred head of beef cows, with each on average generating seven-hundred ninety-two pounds of grass fed, free range and organic beef per year under normal circumstances, generating a combined ninety-six million dollars annually as well as covering all costs while housing, employing and feeding at least five hundred forty formerly homeless persons.

It is certainly reasonable to be curious as to how the foundation managed to acquire so many of these landed properties over that five-year interval. I would like to say, "Oh, it was easy." But alas, that would not be true. What is true is that I can explain the how of it.

You see, there is this federal government action called BRAC, which stands for Base Realignment and Closure, is the congressionally authorized process, as part of the Federal Property Administrative Services Act of 1949. The Department of Defense has used this to reorganize its base structure to more efficiently and effectively support our forces; increase operational readiness; and facilitate new ways of doing business. The process was created by legislation in 2005 to review all military related properties owned by the Department of Defense and determine the value of renovation, or disposal of those not being fully used. A two-part report was released by the Secretary of Defense on May 13, 2005, and published in the Federal Register. It reported evaluations based on criteria developed by the Department of Defense and a summary of the results determined by this application. Projections for the subsequent twenty years included conversion of use, upgrades, transfers as well as disposal of properties. There were five individual rounds of the BRAC process Conducted between 1988 and 2005 that resulted in either closure or reallocation of more than three-hundred federal installations yielding more than ten billion dollars annually in taxpayer funds savings.

Upon the initial discovery by our legal and executive staff, we pursued qualification to bid on any of these federal properties that might be offered for sale.

We met with surprising results based on the advice that Bridgette offered as to what the winning bids would be. You guessed it; she somehow manages to come up with just the right bid to win the purchases without spending too much of our growing funds.

Among these federal properties we have acquired through this BROC process is first, Fort McClellan, Alabama, which was an Army post put into use in 1898, used as an Army recruit training center, a specialty center for the Army chemical corps and chemical warfare training, the training of the Women's Army Corps and military police training command.

After the official closing in 1999, Fort McClellan was used for training by the Alabama National Guard and as the home the U. S. Customs and Border Protections as well as the Center for Domestic Preparedness.

Since the base was formerly a storage site for chemicals munitions it was necessary for substantial maintenance preparations in order to make the property saleable. Finally, the fort was officially cleared of all ordinance and chemicals in 2014 and parcels of property were made available for sale and a section of the original nine thousand acres was transferred to the U.S. Fish and Wildlife Service. Ingener8 Agronomics purchased nearly two-hundred acres and five building.

That initial acquisition was followed shortly by the purchase of a former Naval installation. located on the Cooper River in historic North Charleston, SC, the Charleston Naval Shipyard began operating in 1901. Over the ninety-five-year history of the base, this facility saw the construction of twenty-one destroyers. After World War II, Charleston was homeport for cruisers, destroyers, attack submarines, and more until it was officially closed in 1996. After its closing, the shipyard was leased by a private company that used the dry docks, floating dock, and six piers to service military, commercial, and cruise ships. Today, a portion of the original base is now a multi-use federal complex for up to 17 different agencies including the Coast Guard, Training Centers for Federal Law Enforcement Training Centers and the National Oceanic and Atmospheric Administration. There is also a plan to create mix-use urban properties. Acting as a contributor and participant in that mixed-properties program, our group has secured twenty-eight acres and four buildings for residential and agricultural activities there.

A third and fourth properties became parts of our holdings and operations the next year.

Number three added New York City to our expanding operations. Based on 2020 Census numbers, NYC ranks number one in homeless population in the US with Nearly eighty thousand homeless. In that same year the combined five boroughs of New York City also ranked number one for public school systems in the US with over eighteen-hundred schools serving more than a million students. The New York City Department of Education has in recent years been involved in political battles for control over public school facilities as well as financial management of the system. In NYC two school facilities was priced for quick sale. One on Elmira Avenue, a former middle school on two acres with thirty-eight thousand square feet on four floors, masonry structure. The facility is tax assessed at sixty-five thousand dollars and listed for sale at only fifty-thousand dollars. The second is a former secondary school on Spruce Park Drive consisting of forty-four thousand square feet masonry and steel construction on four point eight acres assessed at one hundred twenty thousand dollars and listed for sale at one hundred ten thousand dollars.

Number three had us bouncing once again to the west coast. Los Angeles city and LA county California at a total count of over sixty-three thousand homeless, ranks the area at number two in the United States according to census numbers.

The US department of education has reported on the impact of a general exodus from California resulting from increases in the purchase and leasing costs of residential real estate as witnessed by legislation passed in 2018 based on what the bill identifies as California's affordable housing crisis, and a decline in business generally has shown a steady decrease in public school enrollment since 2005. Based on reporting of the California Department of Finance, the impact has resulted in six-hundred twenty-five thousand fewer students enrolling in traditional California public schools. It is the hope of that state foundation that the sale of some of the affected properties will help create some cash inflow to assist in other areas for the affected schools.

At the time of our most recent presentation to the board, The Los Angeles Unified School District had over twenty thousand buildings housing over seventy-five million square feet of interior space, the equivalent of seventeen hundred acres. Additionally, the combined properties include over six thousand acres of land. The purchase of four of these school facilities will provide space for housing upward to three thousand individuals plus indoor growing space as well as outdoor open range space for chicken and egg production.

Among the holdings of the LA Unified School District, several school properties were available, including Grace Ferguson High School in Huntington Park, a five-story facility of thirty-five thousand square feet with athletic fields, parking lots and two greenhouses all on fourteen point eight acres. A purchase was negotiated at a cost of six hundred thirty-three thousand five hundred dollars. Built in 1946, It was removed from service in 2009. A second property there was the former George Royce High School Built in 1928 and closed in 2009. Brick and mortar totaling twenty-one thousand square feet on three floors and sitting on three point six five acres. That tract was purchased for two hundred seventy-one thousand six hundred ninety dollars.

As you may have already guessed, the board was more than willing to indulge in these suggested expansions. These purchases as well as the funds used for the acquisitions of these properties was all handled by our board members, Mike and Mary Martha Porter and has been designated for use with our homeless veterans program.

After we were able to find so much success, one morning, while sitting in my office, I could suddenly smell the bountiful fragrance of dark roast coffee. Since it was so early in the morning, I realized that it must mean that Bridgette had quietly slipped into the office kitchen. She is always dependable for a fresh jug of coffee if none has been made prior to her arrival. Just as if by magic after only seconds, she came into my office with her impish grin shining and a steaming mug in each hand. She gently placed one on the desk right in front of me while taking her seat across from me. It was immediately obvious that she was eager to share something other than coffee with me.

"Good morning, Beeep. What's on your mind?"

"Are you getting' mind reading abilities now too?"

"Not really mind reading, maybe just expression reading."

"That's good! Especially when you're right."

"Is it something you can share?"

"Oh, yeah! You know, back year before last, when Kim did all that legal research and got us qualified as a charitable organization and put us on the list of potential buyers for surplus real estate?"

"Yeah, our second year after we created the executive group."

She nodded affirmatively.

"Well, I was thinking that there are many other sources that probably do the same sort of thing. And then I remembered that we actually bought our first farm building here in town for the back taxes owed by the previous owner. Plus, our first residential building was a former public school that was no longer being used.

"And you know, my brother, Jacob is really good at online research. I decided to suggest an idea or two to him to see what he might find.

"And guess what?"

"You're far better at that whole guessing game than I am."

"Duh! You're actually guessing. Not me. I already know the answers."

"Oh, sure! And someday you're gonna tell me how you do that, right?"

"Eh, pro'ly not!"

That reply was followed by that patented giggle.

"But I will tell you what we found. You'll be amazed.

"Based on 2002 census results, there are about fifteen thousand Public School Districts in the US. Combined, these school districts own over ninety-seven thousand School buildings, of which approximately sixty-seven thousand are elementary schools and thirty thousand are secondary schools which tend to have more rooms as well as greater square footage and are on larger tracts of land which will normally include athletic fields and parking lots. On average, about two per cent of these facilities will fall from use each year, owing to declining enrollment or insufficient funds for maintenance and upkeep, resulting in the efforts by the school districts attempting to sell them. That means that in any given year nearly two thousand school facilities and the surrounding grounds in the US are available for purchase, or about forty in each of the fifty states."

"Wow! Let's have him research cities and states where homelessness is a substantial problem and create some sort of ranking spreadsheet that has those stats along with any of these school facilities available in those localities. Then we take that to the executive management group to develop a plan to assist those localities."

"And tell Jake, I said, "Good Job!"

"Sure, but you should know, I already told him you would say that!"

She stood to leave, but I had one more quick question first.

"So, tell me Bridgette, what are you going to do after we solve this whole homelessness problem?"

She spun and grinned at me.

"Well, I'll do it all again. It will need to be done by then.

"I mean, the homeless problem we're working on is just a symptom of the real problem. The real problem that must be fixed or we will need to do this for every generation."

"And the real problem is?"

"Inequality.

Six weeks later, I called a meeting of the board for consideration of our emergency housing project. Jacob, Colt and Bridget had put together some incredible support for adding this new operation to our present bag of tricks. They were even more eager to pursue the acquisition and conversion of more school properties for use for homeless populations. It was agreed upon to order those purchases and program developments based on the locations and numbers of homeless populations creating folks in need.

With the research Jacob and Colt had conducted, they built data bases that easily showed where the needs were, and their resulting priority assignments gave a clear beginning for us to address.

Bridgette offered her own report to me as we stood in my office.

"I'll run through the stats that support these services as well as the basic scheme we might follow in order to have the greatest impact at the front end of this expansion.

"New York City ranks number one in homeless population in the US with nearly eighty thousand homeless according to census numbers for 2020.

"In that same year the combined five boroughs of New York City also ranked number one for public school systems in the US with over eighteen hundred schools serving more than a million students.

"The New York City Department of Education has, in recent years been involved in political battles for control over public school facilities as well as financial management of the system. In the city, two school facilities were priced for quick sale. One on Elmira Avenue, a former middle school on two acres and with thirty-six thousand square feet on four floors, in a masonry structure. The facility is assessed at sixty-five thousand dollars and listed for sale at only fifty thousand eight hundred fifty dollars.

"Second is a former secondary school on Spruce Park Drive consisting of forty-five thousand square feet is a masonry and steel structure on almost five acres assessed at one-hundred eighteen thousand dollars and listed for sale at one-hundred ten thousand dollars.

"Then, there is Los Angeles city and LA county California at a total count of over sixty-three thousand homeless, ranks the area at number two in the US.

"The US department of education has reported on the impact of a general exodus from California resulting from increases in the purchase and leasing costs of residential real estate as witnessed by legislation passed in 2018 based on what the bill identifies as California's affordable housing crisis, and a decline in business generally has shown a steady decrease in public school enrollment since 2005. Based on reporting of the California Department of Finance, the impact has resulted in six-hundred twenty-five thousand fewer students enrolling in traditional California public schools.

"It is the hope of that state foundation that the sale of some of the affected properties will help create some cash inflow to assist in other areas for the affected schools.

At this time of her review of the findings for my presentation to the board, Beeep also informed me that several school properties were available, including Grace Ferguson High School in Huntington Park, a four-story facility of Thirty-two thousand square feet with athletic fields, parking lots and two greenhouses all on Fourteen point eight acres. The listed price was five-hundred thirty thousand five hundred dollars. Built in 1946, It was removed from service in 2009. A second property listed at three-hundred ten thousand dollars was the former George Royal High School Built in 1928 and closed in 2009. Brick and mortar totaling twenty-one thousand square feet on three floors and sitting on three point sixty-five acres.

"These two schools were purchased for a combined two-hundred ninety-one thousand six-hundred ninety dollars! And that isn't even the great part. The buildings and grounds were bought and paid for by our board members Doctor and Mrs. Porter.

"What? How do you know that?"

Her sheepish grin bloomed brightly.

"Well, I may have suggested it!'

"And just like that, they bought them?"

"Well, sure. And they also have bought a fair chunk of Fort Ord, but that is restricted to at least half for homeless veterans."

"Holy Cow Beeep!"

At the time of my presentation to the board, The Los Angeles Unified School District had over twenty thousand buildings housing over seventy-five million square feet of interior space, which is the equivalent of seventeen-hundred acres of floor space. Additionally, the properties were located on just over six-thousand acres of land. The purchase of four of these school facilities would provide space for housing upward to three thousand individuals as well as indoor growing space. Then there is also an outdoor open range space for chicken and egg production.

<> ♦ <>

The following day, I was pleased to share the news of the board's approval with the entire office. There were also specific compliments for a job well done for those present who had spearheaded the school conversion program expansion. Jake, Colt and Bridgette were all excited and encouraged.

One lesson that often repeats itself is that Beeeep's mind is always running at full throttle, even when she appears to be on the verge of slipping into a surprise nap.

"Oh, and another idea I had. You know that my Grandpapa was a career fireman, right?"

"Ah, yeah. He was my brother, afterall!'

"Oh yeah, that's right! Well, what I would like to do is create a temporary housing network in as many places as possible that will provide a roof over head with beds and a kitchen as temporary homes for people and families who lose their homes to fire.

"And we can charge some minimal rent and utilities depending on the kind of fire insurance coverage they have. That would help us with operating costs."

"Hey, I really like that idea. Can you and Jake do the research and develop a presentation for the next board meeting?"

"Okay. I'll talk to him and to Colt as well. I'm sure he would be the best person to create the maintenance numbers for those residences."

"Super!"

"Oh, and Wick, Can I select the name for that operation? I'd like it to be called the DCC-Memorial Firefighter Emergency Housing Project."

'Oh yeah! I love that! Get together with the guys and create a skeletal plan and I'll call an extra board meeting and I will present it for you.

Chapter Fourteen

It was at our next regularly scheduled board meeting, just over two weeks later that I introduced Bridgette's latest service expansion ideas. Since Bridgette and I had first talked about the idea of being able to provide temporary housing with appliances and necessary furnishings to accommodate a family who were forced from their home as a result of fire, we had again conducted research to support the concept of creating this kind of facility and I had been shocked by the numbers. My brother David had been a career first responder as a professional fire fighter and EMT, who was also Bridgette's Grandfather. She had the initial idea and wanted the organization to be named in a manner that would honor his memory.

The research to support the idea of the services yielded surprising results. Until I received the report, I had not even realized that this problem even existed, let alone the magnitude of it.

A major source of the information collected, came from The National Fire Protection Association (NFPA). "NFPA is a non-profit founded in 1896 for the purposes of eliminating death, injury, property and economic loss due to fire and related hazards." (1)

What we found in this research is that fire departments, professional and volunteer combined respond to over three hundred fifty thousand house fires in the average year, or over 7000 in each state. These fires cause more than seven billion dollars in damage.

Even when the residence is only damaged by fire, the family living in that house may need temporary housing for several weeks up to several months. Considering the fact that even though the average core family size has declined from an average of just over 3 members to two and a half members today, there is still the ideal need for two bedrooms to adequately accommodate a necessary living arrangement.

Barbara Stephens joined our board during the conversion of our first agro-garden building. Barb has a BS in construction engineering and an MBA. She has worked in major construction as a project manager, contracts administrator for more than ten years. She became the general manager of Regis Stephens Construction Management, a company she and her husband, Regis, founded.

We first became acquainted with her skill set when we hired her to manage all construction contracts for Ngener8. Their company works as a private project manager for individuals or small companies who are involved in major construction, renovation, or repair. We rely on Barb to ask all the necessary and appropriate questions whenever a new project is proposed. Questions are raised and answered, or good ideas arise as to further research.

We presented our initial plans for the temporary housing for fire victims which faced smooth sailing. The board once again approved the proposed expansion of services by a large margin. It was suggested that an evaluation be done to select up to twelve locations to begin the expansion and to perhaps create a projection for up to fifty locations to be added over the next ten years.

For the DCC Firefighter Emergency Housing Project The logo is a red fireman's helmet with a gold badge on the front with DCC across the center of the badge.

Each residential facility will consist of just under a thousand square feet, housing two bedrooms, one and a half baths, and Kitchen w/Stacked washer and dryer in closet, a living and dining area. One bedroom will have built-in bunk beds and one will have a built-in Queen plus each will have a closet with drawers and built-in desk. situated on about eight thousand square feet of lot or just under a fifth of an acre. Each house will have a four-room terrace apartment duplicating the main floor layout. A paved parking apron large enough for two cars will be done in the front yard of each house and a similar pad at the terrace apartment. The cost of each house will be approximately one hundred fifty-five thousand three-hundred dollars initially when we start the project, and each will generate an average of between twelve thousand five-hundred dollars and nineteen-thousand two-hundred dollars per year. That means the combined revenue can recover the cost of each project location in just eight to ten years.

At this point in the presentation, Barbara Stephens interjected a valuable addition for consideration.

"Might I offer a suggestion? I have done project management with Continental Homes. They do factory-built houses based on any floor plan that might be offered. The cost is about twenty percent less than stick building on the lot and the quality is far more consistent. We might even arrange a contractual agreement with them to build multiple units each year, thereby helping them to keep costs down and passing a portion of those savings on to us."

Instantly Blue Morgan, based, I would guess on his active involvement in corporate development, raised a genuine concern and potentially an expanded addition of services we might consider offering. He said,

"I read an article a few days ago about minimum wage earners not being able to afford to rent an apartment in the United States. Is that something we might look into?

"If, when we buy lots to build these homes, might we purchase three quarters of an acre which based on today's proposal would be adequate to build four of these residences. We use two apartments for the fire emergency housing and the remaining six as low-income units. We could probably find a source for subsidizing the additional units."

"I think that is a really good idea Wick! You might also investigate section eight housing with The Housing and Urban Development Foundation of the federal government."

I was totally flabbergasted and had no informed answer to that question. It did, however, intrigue me. Six or eight adjacent residences (four houses) will use less than three-quarters of an acre and five houses ten-unit models will take a full acre. Each house will have an eight-room main floor and terrace level. We should build these units in larger metropolitan areas as the eight-to-ten-unit model and in smaller areas as the two or four unit. Build at least one facility in as many places as possible. We will work with Continental Homes, a factory manufacturer of modular housing and with multiple insurance companies who provide homeowners insurance.

As is relatively normal for this type of information sharing, there are many questions that inevitably arise. This meeting was perfectly normal in that regard. I actually like it when questions come up. The nature of the question tells me if the board member is really paying attention. And on many occasions, a member's insight is spot on creating an area to be properly researched.

On this date, the thoughts shared by two board members forced me to acknowledge their positive involvement.

"Those are some exceptional ideas and ones which certainly fall into alignment with our present services.

"I'll have the research done and bring an evaluation to our next meeting."

And so, it started, another potential expansion of services for our organization. Our normal board meetings are quarterly, so I had three months to do the research and write a program design that can cover the low-income housing issue.

Four weeks later at our next regularly scheduled meeting, I had some additional and very good information that resulted from research provoked by those comments and suggestions that had come from that earlier meeting.

I was prepared to report what my research had yielded with regards to Section Eight housing assistance. But even before I could share my good news, Barbara Stephens reported on a consultation she had instigated with Continental Homes. I eagerly allowed her to have the floor first.

"I suggested in our last meeting that I have worked on numerous occasions with Continental Homes. Since they offer Dealer franchises to many construction companies around the nation, I approached them with our ideas of building their homes for use as temporary housing for the Firefighter project.

"For those unfamiliar, let me tell you a bit about Continental. I'm sure you are all aware that there are manufactured homes. But what you may not realize is that there are multiple types of manufactured homes.

"The most widely known and familiar category here is the mobile home. Or as we called them when I was a kid, trailers.

"In the trade, houses built on site are referred to as stick-built. There are also manufactured houses that are stick-built, but in a factory on an assembly line much like cars and trucks. Then they are transported in sections or modules to a prepared foundation on the site, assembled, plumbed, wired, and otherwise finished.

"What you end up with there is basically a stick-built house at a substantially lower cost per square foot. A win-win if you will.

"Over the past week and a half, I have negotiated with Continental to build multiples of these homes for us. What I have managed to do is in effect get us a discount based on the number of homes we buy from them in one-year segments. And if we order multiples in a single order, we will get the discounts with that order. In effect we will be granted a franchise for their homes and in so doing, receive a discount of sixteen and two thirds percent as do their dealers.

"The basic unit is the model nine seventy-two which retails for one hundred forty thousand five hundred dollars. Our cost for the two-bedroom bath and a half, Living-room and kitchen house will be one hundred seventeen thousand twenty-five dollars and that includes the partitions, floors and other necessary prefab segments for the terrace apartment as well. Where we are unable to have a useable basement owing to soil density issues that cost will decline by twenty-three thousand seventy-five dollars.

"Then Stephens Contracting will do the installation and completion on site. Other related costs per house for connecting the dwelling to the foundation, electric service, water and sewage, paving, sidewalks and landscaping another eighty-five hundred dollars. The cost for pickup and delivery with American Veterans Transfer is dependent on the location where the units will be installed.

"Now I'll yield the floor to our CEO who has a report on land purchases and other related information."

"Thank you Barbara. Last week I returned from a trip out west. I enlisted our board members Mary Martha and Mike Porter to assist in the review and negotiations for the purchase of land tracts in multiple states to be used for our residential programs.

"We were successful in the acquisition of

I was also astounded that I would be able to report to the board that we had purchased $1,100,000 of land value, without spending any of the foundation's capital.

Mike Porter had donated more than half that amount and for the remainder, he had successfully solicited corporate and private donations.

Chapter Fifteen

I truly like what I am doing these days and am particularly pleased when things go smoothly as the most recent board meeting had done. After that meeting I had gone to lunch with my Vice president for finance. John and I have been good friends since graduate school. We were even in each other's weddings and had shared an apartment briefly.

We decided to go to one of our old haunts, so it was not surprising that we crossed paths with other folks we had known for a while.

This path crossing would turn out to be mutually beneficial for our organization as well as our old friend, John Star. The old friend had owned an auto repair shop that John Viken and I had used since those days of old. He had left the shop and became a long-haul trucker.

"So, how's the truckin' doin'?"

"It's going great! In fact, I just bought my third tractor along with a forty-foot refrigerated trailer. My son, Jimmy, got out of the Marine Corp. a few months ago, and we decided to open our own company."

He proudly handed me a business car that was on white stock and printed in red and blue. The company was printed to look like a waving flag with the name "American Veterans Transfer/Trucking" with a line across the bottom below names Jimmy Star on the left side and John Star on the right. The line on the bottom was a dark blue that ran through a slogan oriented in red. It said, "No Load Too Big or Small".

Instantly it occurred to me that with our beef, chicken meat, egg and vegetable operations all over the country that our organization could benefit from a contract with a company who could handle all shipping.

When I shared my ideas with John Star, he all but turned a back flip. And a new business relationship was born.

Chapter Sixteen

It has been a busy couple of months. I contacted Mary Martha and asked if she could join me, with her airplane to do some real estate travelling. When I explained about my idea to visit some metropolitan areas where we wanted to start our fire emergency housing projects, she said,

"Absolutely! I was really happy to read the minutes from the last board meeting about that expansion of services. I'm sorry Mike and I were not able to attend but gave my vote privileges to Mal Barrett. Ans since the vote was unanimous, I can see that she must have vote in favor, which is exactly what I would have done.

"Will you email me the places you want to visit so I can put together a flight plan?"

"I will do that. I'm wondering if I should fly out there to meet you and start in your area. Know a good realtor?"

"Yes, I do. My neighbor and one of my best friends is a partner with her husband in a real estate firm. Tell me what we're going to be looking for and I get started. When do you want to do this?'

"Well, it's Thursday and I was thinking that I could take a redeye on Monday morning. How would that be for you?"

"If you book a flight into Seattle-Tacoma International and email me the flight number and I'll meet you there."

"I'll also send you the several places I'd like to visit to see potential property purchases."

First thing on Friday morning, my plan was to draft an email to Mae Mae sharing my plans and property needs with her.

Just as I sat down in my office, there was a gentle tapping at my door. Even before I answered, I had little doubt as to who was there.

"Come in Bridgette."

The door opened only inches and that sweet face poked through with a grin.

"I take it you're putting together you land list for your trip to Washington."

"Yep. Do you need something?"

"No. Actually, you do."

"Yeah, what's that?"

Bridgette without even knowing where he plans to visit offers some information.

"In Seattle see either Connie or Alfred Collins. They own Collins Realty.

"When you're in Reno, Nevada give Garnett or Garland Garcia a call. He is a potential land doner. As chairman and CEO of 4G construction, he controls land owned by the company and is a strong supporter of homeless and veterans projects.

"There is a developer in Wyoming named Calvin Grossman (Cal to his friends) who wants to help with a project

"Oh and forget about Oakland or LA at present. The land costs there are through the moon. We'll find a doner there after we build enough of these units elsewhere.

Our basic property needs are completely straight forward in that we desire to purchase a residential lot or lots that are at least eight thousand square feet or multiples of that square footage and with zoning for multiple occupancy residential structures on each lot potentially.

Now with the insights Beeep had offered, I could share more information in my email. I created an email with a proposed itinerary along with what I'd just gotten from my co-founder.

I also gave her a description of the number of municipalities I'd like to visit ideally depending on her schedule availability.

And finally, I booked my flight from Dulles to Seattle and owing to the very early departure time of that flight, I also made a hotel reservation on the Dulles compound for Sunday night.

My Monday morning flight departed Dulles at 6:00 am and arrived at Seattle/Tacoma at 14 minutes after noon local time. After the nine and a quarter hour flight, I met Mary Martha and, for the first time, her husband Mike, at the passenger terminal and she said we were meeting her neighbor and friend Connie for lunch.

"Might that be Connie Collins?"

"Do you know her?"

"Do she and her husband, Alfred own Collins Real Estate?"

"Okay, now I'm totally confused or maybe just impressed. How do you know them?"

"Well, the truth is that I don't. I mean I was told about them, but that's another story. I'll try to explain later."

Since I was just along for the ride, I just left the choice to my hostess when she asked if I had any preference as to restaurant.

"Okay. We have a great place that Mike and I both love. It's called Thirteen Coins and is right here on International Blvd. We can either eat inside or my favorite is to have patio seating."

"That sounds nice. Does the name have anything to do with pricing?"

Mary Martha laughed aloud.

"Ah, no. It is from an old Spanish myth about a love-sick young man who was just a poor worker who fell madly in love with the boss's daughter. When he asked for her hand in marriage and Dad asked what the young man could offer, the boy held out his hand and said" this and my eternal love, care and support." In his hand were thirteen coins. It was all that he had in the world. The father was so impressed that he approved of the marriage.

"Now there is even a marriage ceremony in the Spanish Catholic Church called thirteen coins! It symbolizes absolute love and caring."

"Wow. And this restaurant is named for that?"

"Yep."

We waited for Connie to come in and then we were seated on the patio. Mary Martha made the introductions as her realtor friend arrived.

Hey Connie! This is my old high school friend, Wick Blair. Wick, this is my friend Connie Collins."

"Pleasure to meet you, Wick. I understand that you're in the market for some pieces of land in multiple cities."

"Yes, our foundation is planning to build housing units in a dozen or more cities in the northwest, then we are planning to spread out further."

"Yeah, Mary Martha sent me your list last Friday. I've got several properties in several Cities."

We took our seats on the patio. Each of us was given a menu. It was a totally unusual and fascinating menu too. Since it was my first meal of the day, I selected Dungeness Crab Omelette with hashbrowns and toast.

Connie said that after lunch, we had several properties scheduled for a visit and review. During our meal I was pleased that Connie asked many questions about our organization and our planned projects.

It gave me the opportunity to include Mike, as a member of our board without making it sound boastful.

Connie also informed me that her firm was a member of a national franchise, and she could call upon other franchise members in the several cities I had told Mary Martha about in my email to her earlier. Connie offered to be the realtor representing our organization and join Mary Martha and me on our tour circuit.

The true surprise was when Mike offered to take the day off and act as our pilot.

"Thanks, Mike, that would be great."

"I also figured that with two pilots along, we can take the Gulfstream."

After lunch, Connie took us in her minivan to see a few properties in the Seattle-Tacoma area. What was amazing is that we found two nearly ideal options among four that we viewed. The first of those was a one point one sixty-four-acre plot on Union Avenue listed at one hundred twenty-five thousand dollars. I signed contract with an offer of one hundred twelve thousand five hundred dollars. This piece of property could accommodate nine residential house units and at my offer would be twelve thousand dollars per unit. The second plot located on South 130th Street was already a good deal at an asking price of only forty-nine thousand nine hundred ninety-seven dollars for one point oh nine acres. I signed a contract offering forty-eight thousand dollars which would allow for six house units at eight thousand dollars for each lot.

Then in Tacoma, on east 45th Street there was a one point thirteen-acre tract listed at one hundred five thousand dollars. This piece of land would handle six residential structures. Here, on the advice from Connie, I signed an offer of ninety thousand dollars giving us a land cost of fifteen thousand dollars per residential unit.

The huge success that first day was that Mike Porter asked if he could buy the property and donate it to the organization!

Over the next five days, we flew from Seattle-Tacoma to Portland Oregon then Boise, Idaho and then onto Casper and Cheyenne Wyoming and to Reno and finally Las Vegas, Nevada. The final leg was back to Seattle-Tacoma on Friday afternoon.

Throughout the course of my western travels, I committed to six more land purchases, acquiring adequate building sites to construct one hundred twenty-three houses with each accommodating two residential spaces each in a total of five states, Washington, Oregon, Idaho, Montana, and Nevada.

I was very pleased with my results as notice of acceptance of the offers I'd made. My next project would take me to several other states, but as we were landing that Friday evening, I was more than pleased when Mike and Mary Martha told me of their intentions to fly me back to Virginia and to work with me to help with several more land shopping trips.

On Friday we met again at the airport and departed at just after seven in the morning. Mike had filed a flight plan with a destination of Roanoke-Blacksburg Regional airport. The two-thousand-mile flight took just over six hours and had us landing just after ten am EDT.

While Mike and Mary Martha were getting the jet into a hanger, I arranged the rental of a Dark blue Cadillac Escalade for the sixty-five-mile drive back home. This expenditure, I paid personally.

I invited the Porters to be guests at my home and we spent the weekend consuming some sorely needed rest and relaxation.

During our weekend around the pool, I received a video call from our west coast realtor Connie. She was eager to let me know that properties had not only been acquired in Arizona, but corporate donations Connie and her husband had successfully solicited had covered the costs of them. It came as quite a surprise when I learned that the donor was none other than a member of our board.

"Wick, I'm so excited to tell you that we purchased two tracts in Arizona. On Irving Street in Phoenix, we were successful with an offer of sixty-nine thousand five-hundred dollars for two point thirty-five acres which at one hundred two thousand six hundred-fifty square feet, this tract will accommodate thirteen residential units with a land cost for each of fifty-three hundred forty-seven dollars. In Flagstaff we acquired forty acres. It was suggested by the donor who paid for both properties that you might use thirty-five acres for a cattle ranch and then build twenty-four single residences on the remaining five acres.

"They would have to have only the upper units since the soil will not accommodate a basement.

"The price for that tract was ninety thousand dollars."

"Now wait. This donor, is whom?"

"Oh, Yale Waterman who identified himself as a member of your board."

"Oh, yes, Yale is on our board. And he paid for these two purchases?"

"Yes, he gave me what he called a blank check for up to one hundred seventy-five thousand dollars. Was that okay?'

I was completely flabbergasted, but thankful.

"How much was the total of asking pieces."

"That was one hundred ninety thousand dollars. My husband and I negotiated them down."

"Thanks Connie. And please thank your husband for me as well."

Chapter Seventeen

Our regular board meeting was still four weeks into the future. But we had done so much activity for the foundation that a report to the board was sorely needed, if not past due. So, I called an interim meeting for Tuesday of next week. That will allow me six days to get my report organized. My plans include reporting of the purchase of land in ten western cities. I also want to include information about our arrangement with Continental Homes and with American Veterans Transfer & Trucking to move the houses.

With my plan and dozens of pages listing the specific details, I took the floor at that specially called meeting,

"Good morning fellow board members and thank you for meeting on this relatively short notice. Let me save time and get right to the reasons for our get together.

"As you may know, I have just returned from a trip to the northwest. Courtesy of Mary Martha and Mike Porter, I was able to visit ten cities in six states and had a modicum of success making acquisitions totaling just over sixteen acres for a combined net cost to the foundation of zero.

"These purchases are sufficient to build forty houses with a total of sixty-seven units at an average net land cost per unit of ... well zero!

"Properties in Seattle and Tacoma were donated by our realtor there. Then we bought a two-acre plat in Portland, at one hundred seventy-five thousand dollars. That purchase can accommodate eleven houses or twenty-two units at a unit cost of seventy-nine hundred fifty-four dollars for land. Next we purchased just under an acre and a quarter in Boise Idaho for seventy-nine thousand dollars. That can handle six houses for twelve units at sixty-five hundred eighty-three dollars per unit for land.

"Then the real fun started in Casper, Wyoming, where we met a new friend and doner by the name of Calvin Grossman. There, with Cal's help, I was able to buy forty acres for sixty-nine thousand nine hundred dollars, then sold thirty-six of those acres to Cal, who is a developer there with whom we agreed in advance to a mutual working deal. Cal bought thirty-six of those acres for sixty-nine thousand, leaving us four acres at a net cost of nine hundred dollars. That property will allow us to build sixteen 16 houses with thirty-two units giving each unit a land cost of twenty-eight dollars and thirteen cents!

"Next, we were able to do a very similar deal with the same developer. Our purchase price for seven acres in Cheyenne, Wyoming was sixty-nine thousand nine hundred dollars. We then sold six acres for sixty thousand five-hundred dollars, leaving us one acre for only ninety-four hundred bucks. That will accommodate six houses or twelve units at a net cost of seven hundred eighty-three dollars per unit land cost.

"We then headed to Nevada. In Reno, we were able to procure just over twelve acres for seventy-seven thousand dollars. We then sold ten acres for seventy-two thousand five hundred dollars. This transaction was approved in advance as to the purchase of the portion that we sold leaving slightly over two acres at a net cost of forty-seven hundred fifty dollars. The remaining parcel is enough for eleven houses, with a total of twenty-two units at an average land cost of two hundred sixteen dollars.

"Finally, we went on to Las Vegas where land is more expensive as one would certainly guess. There we found one hundred two point six four acres that was listed for six hundred sixty-four thousand nine hundred dollars. The deal arranged with the Garcia brothers and 4-G allowed us to buy the tract and to sell one hundred acres to the brothers Construction group for six hundred thousand, leaving us two point six four acres. That is enough land for fourteen of our houses with twenty-eight units at twenty-three-hundred eighteen dollars per unit land cost.

"In the case of these two buys in Nevada, the pre-arranged deals were done through agreements with Garrison and Garland Garcia arranged with a simple telephone call. The Garcia brothers were determined to be potential land doners. As chairman and CEO and CFO of 4G construction, they control all land owned or acquired by the company and both are strong supporters of homeless and veterans projects. To go even a step further, this purchase was funded by these doners, Garnett and Garland Garcia are both veterans. I contacted the brothers on advice from our co-founder Bridgette.

"I should also, at this point, give due credit to Bridgette who also helped in making the arrangements with Calvin Grossman in Wyoming and in Reno, Nevada.

"I returned last week and shortly after my arrival back at the office, our west coast realtor, Connie called to tell me of the purchase of two more parcels.

"Those purchases were in Phoenix Arizona where a two point three five- acre parcel was made for sixty-nine thousand five hundred dollars to allow for 13 residential house units. Owing to non-density of the desert soil, these houses will not allow basements so no double count on those units.

"Additionally, in Flagstaff, we were able to secure ten and a half acres at a cost of seven hundred ninety-nine thousand and then through a pre-arranged deal, sold nine and a half acres for that full seven hundred ninety-nine thousand with one acre remaining for six houses with twelve units and a net land cost of zero per unit for both Arizona locations. This zero-cost resulted because our Seattle realtor along with a developer in Flagstaff agreeing in advance to the sale/buy process with transaction costs covered in full by donation from Seattle real estate husband/wife owners.

"That trip and the resulting purchases and sales and donations resulted in the following:

At this point, I shared an overhead image from my laptop, which included the following chart:

In Seattle – 9 buildings =18 units
In Tacoma – 6 buildings = 12 units
In Portland – 11 buildings = 22 units
In Boise – 8 buildings = 16 units
In Casper – 5 buildings = 10 units

In Cheyenne – 8 buildings = 16 residential units.
In Reno – six buildings = 6 units.
In Las Vegas - 11 buildings = 22 units
In NE Albuquerque- 12 buildings = 24 units.

"**O**ur founding Board Member Bridgette advised us that in SW Albuquerque, land is dirt-cheap, but temps are literally HELL.

"Also, in Oakland California, based again on the advice from that co-founding board member, we avoided any purchase at this time until we locate an adequate source of donated funding since Bridgette advised that elevated property prices are prohibitive at this time.

"We will schedule a trip in the future specifically to locate California lands at a practical cost for our purposes.

My presentation was interrupted as Bridgette knocked and opened the door just enough for her slim framed to slide into the board room. She nodded in apology to those of us seated at the meeting table before passing me a single sheet of printer paper. I looked down to see a message that I immediately realized I should share with the Board.

<> ♦ <>

After the meeting was completed and I returned to my office, Bridgette and Colt came into my office.

"Hey Boss, how do you think things went with the board?"

It was Bridgette who raised the question. I had the feeling that the board was interested in what we have planned next. Since these ideas almost always seemed to originate with Beeep, I just turned the tables.

"Let me ask you a question first."

She grinned and nodded as if she already knew what my question was going to be. And based on the little I knew about her, I suspected that she did. Still, I had to ask.

"Now that Ingener8 is up and rapidly growing, what are you planning to do next?"

"Well, I'll do it all again. It will need to be done by then.

"I mean, the homeless problem we're working on is just a symptom of the real problem. The real problem that must be fixed or we will need to do this for every generation."

"And the real problem is?"

"Inequality.

Chapter Eighteen

From our humble beginnings only nine and a half years ago, "Ngener8" Agronomics has grown from a great idea in one community to a national organization operating in seventeen states with forty-five facilities serving over nine thousand homeless persons. At present we are in the process of acquiring additional locations in eight more states.

Our operating budget has grown from $218,000 in that founding year to our projected operating budget for next year at just shy of one hundred million dollars. More importantly, we have relocated and given new life opportunity and meaningful purpose to over twenty-four thousand formerly homeless persons.

I am so often left wondering how it is possible that I, a former college professor, could have even been a part of this effort. And when I drift off in consideration of that miracle, I am often brought back to the reality of it by that sweet giggle and childlike voice of my mentor and guide, none other than Beeep herself.

So, if there are doubts in anyone reading this tale, rest assured that I am just as confused as you. My research has led me to accept the possibility that she truly is the reincarnation of the Irish Saint Bridget. I have no other explanation the holds any water.

Then we must add Uncle Ray or as he initially spelled it simply Ra or Rae. And, to date, all of my research into that historical entity has uncovered the Egyptian Sun God who specialized in bringing the growing season to that region.

"Hey Bridgette, back a few months ago when you and I were talking in the office about adding more school properties, do you remember my asking you what you were going to do next after our success with Ingener8?"

"Yeah, what about it?"

"In response, you said that you'll just have to do it again."

"Yep. That's exactly what I expect to do."

"You went on to say that homelessness is not really the problem, but it's only a symptom of the real problem."

"Yes, that is the case, and it has only grown worse over the years. Even with all the efforts of social programs and groups and organizations like ours, working to treat the illness, the disease has only gotten more rampant.

"Homelessness, hunger, underemployment or unemployment, drug-related crime, crime in general, grossly exacerbated by untrained police officers who think they ARE the law rather than that they only enforce the law.

"We have so many contributing factors. We don't focus nearly enough on education. By properly educating everyone, we could at least reduce ignorance. Ignorance leads to not understanding so much of life.

"This lack of understanding leads then to fear and what we fear, we often end up hating. That hate causes racism, poor people, and more. And religion which should create empathy instead only makes the separation wider."

"Then Bridgette, perhaps you can suggest what you see as the cause, or rather the disease, as you put it, that produces all those symptoms you just listed?"

"Do you have a couple of years? I can explain it all to you."

Here I am the college professor with two doctoral degrees, and I'm being offered a course by a young lady who isn't even a high school graduate ... at least as far as I am aware. Of course, there is much about Bridgette of which I am apparently, no, obviously unaware.

"Take as long as you wish. I am confident I'll be able to keep up."

"By the way, I AM a high school graduate, just in case you weren't sure about that.

"Okay. Let's start with ... oh, a hundred fifty years ago when we were an agricultural economy. The Farm was the business, and the farm workers were the employees. No one was getting rich. Still, both owners and employees had food to eat and a place to sleep.

"Then along comes the industrial revolution. The corporate world was created at that point. Initially, that created an opportunity for a group with a common interest to invest relatively small amounts thereby becoming a part owner of a business they would, otherwise be unable to be involved.

"In it's infancy, the ideas behind this step in the process were positive and could have led to very positive results for everyone involved. Sadly, there were families with far more to invest and when they did invest, their earnings were greater than that of the simple worker.

"This simple inequality led to fewer owners with much larger investments allowing them much greater control in industry and increasing inequality of income.

"There was one positive reaction to this imbalance. The workers realized how they too could force themselves into a better distribution of both control and earnings. They organized labor unions.

"For a fairly good period of time, these unions benefited the working masses. But, as with most everything, the long-term solution didn't really work so well for the long term. Whether it was manufacturing or mining or distribution, each industry was still controlled by the group with most of the wealth. And that group was made up of the majority stockholders. In other words, the owners.

"It was only a matter of time until those owners realized that with their money, they could control regulations and the newly introduced income tax by controlling elected officials.

"The next phase in that developmental journey was the creation of corporate lobbying. Add mergers and the centers of wealth grow at an ever-increasing rate. And let us not forget those family-owned plantations from the agricultural days, that became family-owned corporations where wealth is centered.

"The present result is that there are a limited number of families, plantation owners if you will, and the rest of society is made up of serfs, staff, share-croppers, tenants, and ultimately, slaves.

"The only true difference is the workplace, the products and the appearance of society. And the plantation owners still control who, what, when, where, and how. And worst, they keep education limited and costly to prevent any cultural elevations from happening. Then they use ignorance to generate fear thereby keeping their control.

"They decide if, and when we have wars; what new laws are created, allowing them to continue maintaining control.

"If you look back after the Great Depression, these owners developed company towns where their factories or mines were the singular or at the very least, the major employers and those companies owned the grocery stores, pharmacies, day care centers, health care centers, all of which allowed the employees to have charge accounts, so the working folks were dependent on the company for all aspects of their lives. The working stiffs were figuratively if not literally owned by the company.

"There was even company script used to pay the workers and it was the currency of the company town."

"Bridgette, how in the world do you know all this, let alone understand any of it?"

"Would you believe me if I told you that I've seen it first-hand?

"But how could that be?"

"I can explain it all to you, but I don't know that it is as important as actually addressing the problem."

"And do you have a plan that can do that?"

"Got a few more years?"

"You have both my curiosity and my undivided attention. And that for as long as it takes!"

"If I can give you a rational place to start, will you agree to help me do it?"

"Of course, I will! I trust you totally, Bridgette, you are wise way beyond your years."

"And how do you know that? You have no idea about how many years I am."

I had to admit that she was totally correct, but this allowed me an excuse to pursue that issue as well.

"The simple answer there is for you to tell me all about that."

"I'll have to calculate that for you. You'll agree that experience is both about knowledge and wisdom, right?"

She gave me only a few seconds to consider her suggestion and when I sort of nodded in momentary acceptance, she continued.

"So, for every year I've spent in classrooms, does that add a year to my relative age? Then, what about knowledge which I gain elsewhere, like from reading. I am an avid reader, you know."

"I'm talking about how many years you've been breathing, eating, and thinking. How many of those?"

"This time?"

"What?"

"You know that whole 'old soul' business. You've heard of that, right?"

She didn't even give me a second to think about what she had said before the giggle arrived.

"I'm just one of those!"

Chapter Nineteen

I had not been into the office for nearly a week. After our board meeting, I had been out of town doing a tour of four of our other locations in the state. Colt had given me the tour to see his handy work at renovations of the old buildings.

My work plan for the day was to begin a prioritized list of our plans for the remaining quarter of our fiscal year. I was more than pleased when I saw that Bridgette was sitting at the worktable just outside my office. I would certainly need her help with my list.

"Hey Beeep! I'm glad to see you here."

"I knew you might need me, so I came in. How was your tour?"

"Oh, it was super. I am so glad we have Colt on our team. He just grabs a project by the horns and wrestles it to the ground. And his work is premium."

"I'm glad he joined us too."

"So Beeep, remember when we were prepping for the board meeting last week and you and I were talking about the problem not being homelessness but that being only a symptom of the real problem?"

"Of course, I remember that. I went on to explain it and other related symptoms."

"You also said you have some ideas about fixing the real problem and that you would share those with me as well.

"Oh, and you were also going to answer my question about your age!"

"Which is the most important answer?"

"Both are equally important to me."

She looked me squarely in the eyes for what seemed like an hour, but which was probably no more than ten seconds. I believe that she was deciding what information she would offer. Then she had obviously made her decision.

"As you'll recall, I said that the real problem is inequality. This single difference in our society has a universal impact on our society."

"And I believe that you have some theories about how this should be addressed."

"The right place to start is to work toward having a return to more genuine 'BY the people FOR the people' atmosphere in this country.

"We must Create Term Limits for ALL public offices: having two terms of 4 years each for any single office for life. There must be no private funds used in any election, but rather an equal budget from public funds for each candidate for each office. There must be ABSOLUTELY NO GIFTS, Trips, Entertainment to any office holder or candidate for office. Annual Salary will be 1/2 of the average gross annual income reported on the federal income tax for the ten years prior to election to office plus the current minimum wage calculated for 40 hours per week for 52 weeks. Social Security will be the only provided retirement and Medicare the only health insurance.

"We must create ONE National Police Force that will replace all State, Territory, County, Local police/law enforcement departments. ALL police officers will be required to have at least a BA/BS degree in law/crime/criminal psychology prior to entry into a compulsory law enforcement academy.

"Make ALL education from pre-school through doctoral studies tuition free through public schools and state colleges/universities. And, to encourage students to stay in school, require a high school diploma in order to qualify to test for a driver's license prior to the twenty-fifth birthday.

"And to directly impact the inequality of income, overhaul all Internal Revenue Service codes to create a system that is simple and adequate. Tax rates will be based on gross income steps where everyone with reported income is charged a percentage that begins at three percent up to one thousand dollars per year, five percent at twenty thousand dollars; seven percent at thirty thousand dollars; ten percent at fifty thousand dollars, after which increases at intervals which increase ten percent at one hundred thousand dollars another ten percent followed at two hundred thousand dollars another ten percent; then at three hundred thousand dollars; then again with another ten percent at five hundred thousand dollars and finally another ten percent at seven hundred fifty thousand dollars leaving the highest bracket at seventy-five percent above three quarters of a million total annual income.

"That allows for funding for all needed federal programs and the ability to fund the needed additions like universal healthcare at no cost to the patient; a federal mortgage program that would assist low-income first-time buyers; alternative energy programs like wind, solar and whatever might be discovered later.

"Included might be research and development in areas like alternate power sources for homes, industry, public transit, and automobiles.

"Another field that must be changed is that of privately owned prisons operated for profit. Rather the issue of things like mental health, alcohol, and drug treatment to rehab those convicted of crime.

"Efforts need to be focused on prevention rather than punishment."

I had been forced to take a seat before she had even gotten done with the suggested changes in tax structure. As usual I was totally flummoxed. How does this petite little lady even begin to know so much, let alone understand any of it? Suddenly, the other part of the explanation I had been looking forward to, The one I believed she had agreed to answer at this later time. I was re-visiting my internal debate about how powerfully I should pursue that other issue.

I decided that I just couldn't wait any longer.

"So, Beeep, What about that other question? You know, The one about your age."

"Oh sure, I remember that. I think you have some sort of silly idea that I'm ageless or sumpin'.

"My guess is that you have some kinda wild theory that I'm like Brigit, the **Catholic Saint and Celtic Goddess of Healing. She is the one that Celts have worshipped as a saint and a Goddess since like 1500 years ago. That Brigit was the daughter of Boyann, Goddess of the River Boyne in Ireland. She was known to support the arts, was the guardian of children and animals, had the ability to heal, and most importantly the power of prophecy.**

"If that were true, I'd be like, geez, two-thousand years old! I look way better than that! Right?"

She looked at me with that sweet innocent face, those green eyes twinkling. I felt like she was willing me not to go on with this line of questioning. At the same time, I just knew that she had not made any attempt to answer the question at hand. As usual, she managed to respond to my question without answering it. It seemed that she had more to offer, so **I waited.**

"Now there is one thing she and I do have in common, well, besides similar names, and that is that she created a charitable sort of school for her young followers. It could easily be seen as the idea that started Ingener8.

"At her school, her students during their first few years of residence, attended training classes, after which they spent ten years using what they had been trained for by tending her wells, groves and beds growing and gathering herbs that were farmed for use for their healing properties. They were taught how to care for livestock, and how to forge iron into tools. Their last years were spent teaching others. That's very similar in concept to our homeless residential program. Bridgit was also a protector of all children, and I would certainly be in favor of that!"

She again hesitated, as if she was finished. I just decided to wait her out again. And again, my silence seemed to encourage her to continue.

"The only other possibility is that you might have the even wilder idea that somehow, I am Saint Bridgit reincarnated. And for so many reasons, IF that were somehow the case, then there are multiple reasons that I could not answer that question.

"I mean, first and foremost, I don't know how I could know if I were a reincarnation of some Irish Goddess. Even if I thought that might be the case, couldn't that idea simply be some sort of ego trip?

"I'm just a young woman with ideas. Let's just leave it at that. Please."

Chapter Twenty

At our most recent Board meeting, I opened with an offer to the assembled members who might have something to offer or request.

Our legal department represented by Kim Andrews took the floor.

"Good Thursday morning to each of you. I am most pleased first to have the opportunity to serve as a part of this truly exceptional organization.

"Today, I am more than pleased to advise you that the very personality of this foundation is addictive. Its very nature has caused my law partner and sister, Claire Andrews to seek a way to become a part of this worthy occupation.

"As a result of the knowledge gleaned here, we have made the commitment to take a more active role in the delivery of services to assist a category of those in need.

"Claire and I are in the process of buying 1082 acres in Kennebec County with a contemporary log home with four bedrooms and two baths near Augusta, Maine for eight hundred twenty-nine thousand nine-hundred dollars.

"Our plan is to develop an orchard that will produce and sell organic apples, ciders, and Organic Apple Butter including a no sugar added version. A hotel-like residence hall will be added to accommodate foster children who will receive mental health assistance while learning to work at the orchard. The facility will be called Apple Tree Shelter and in addition to at risk children, it will also be a shelter for abandoned animals, including dogs, cats, horses, and others as well as a boarding facility for animals while owners are travelling etc.

"A full staff will be employed to provide mental health counseling services, academic programs through the high school level including administering GED testing, and more.

"Included in our plan is the construction of a residential facility designed to house at least sixty residents in dorm-like rooms with a dining hall and training space, office space for staff, and a library which will be stocked through solicited book donations by published authors.

"Our initial staffing will be provided through internship programs done in cooperation with multiple universities and colleges in the northeast.

"The facility will be a charter member of the Ingener8 Foundation and initially created and funded by the two of us and our family."

At our most recent regular meeting of the Board, I offered an update on the status of projects as the current plans encompassed.

This was a good meeting to offer this report since, every current board member was present.

"Good morning, and welcome. In less than a full decade The Ingener8 Foundation has made great strides. From our simple and hopeful beginnings, we have grown to a multi-million-dollar annual operating budget. From our two buildings here in the hill city, we have spread our operational sites to more than a dozen states and today's agenda includes projected expansion into even more locations.

"Our budget for the founding year, didn't even exist when we first started operations. For the coming fiscal year, we have a budget of one hundred four million, seven hundred thirty-five thousand dollars. From our one initial donor, we now have four hundred seventy individual and corporate donors and our agro operations generate three hundred thirty-one million nine hundred fifty-two thousand one hundred sixty dollars annually.

"Our plan for the near future is to develop more temporary residences within the DCC Firefighter Emergency Housing Project. We have estimated needs based on studies from fire insurance companies and numbers gleaned from census data. The new residences will be added in a first round, beginning within the next six months in Philadelphia, Pennsylvania; Boston, Massachusetts; Charlotte and Raleigh-Durham, North Carolina; Alexandria, Virginia; Charleston, West Virginia; Baltimore, Maryland.

"This first group will consist of twenty-four houses having a total of ninety-six residential units.

"Then a second round of expansions will begin within twelve months after completion of the first cycle with an additional twenty-four houses with ninety-six residential units and will be located in five cities to include Little Rock, Arkansas; Birmingham and Montgomery, Alabama; Kansas City and Saint Louis, Missouri.

"Another crew will be procuring vacated school buildings and other empty and available buildings that can work for conversion to indoor farming and with the necessary conversion, adding new homeless residences and agronomic farm buildings in Philadelphia, New York City, Boston, Birmingham, Alabama, Kansas City, and Saint Louis.

"With the exception of one small and unanswered question, I would say we are a raving success!"

The End of This Tale for Now, but the Beginning of Some Really Good Ideas